VERCOQUIN AND THE PLANKTON

VERCOQUIN AND THE PLANKTON

———

BORIS VIAN

TRANSLATED BY TERRY BRADFORD

WAKEFIELD PRESS
CAMBRIDGE, MASSACHUSETTS

This book was set in Garamond Premier Pro, Helvetica Neue Pro, and Marilyn Bold by Wakefield Press. Printed and bound by McNaughton & Gunn, Inc., in the United States of America.

ISBN: 978-1-939663-82-5

Available through D.A.P./Distributed Art Publishers
75 Broad Street, Suite 630
New York, New York 10004
Tel: (212) 627-1999
Fax: (212) 627-9484

10 9 8 7 6 5 4 3 2 1

CONTENTS

TRANSLATOR'S INTRODUCTION

Tickling the Toes of Mummies

Boris Vian was born in the suburbs of Paris in 1920. By the time France was liberated from Nazi Occupation, he was a married man and a father with a day job at the Association Française de Normalisation (the national standards organization of France). So far, it would seem, so boring. But he had also written a collection of poems, a fairy tale, and two novels. He was, moreover, an established face on the Franco-Belgian jazz scene—an active member of the Hot Club de France, he played trumpet with Claude Abadie's prize-winning jazz group. When he died just fifteen years later, in 1959, he had written eight further novels, a wealth of short stories, plays, operas, scripts, writings on jazz, chronicles, articles, and other texts, as well as nearly five hundred songs.[1]

In the aftermath of the war, Vian caused a furor with his first published novel *J'irai cracher sur vos tombes* (*I Spit on Your Graves*). Written in fifteen days to win a bet, and published in November 1946, this hoax ("within a hoax . . . within a hoax")[2] became a bestseller.[3] When *Vercoquin et le plancton* appeared in the bookshops of Paris in January 1947, he still had not officially owned up to having himself written the *roman à scandale*.[4] It was in that context, in the words of Marc Lapprand, that *Vercoquin et le plancton* "propelled Boris Vian into the world of letters in a manner as unhoped for as it was relatively sudden."[5] And this was just two months before the publication of the work widely regarded as his masterpiece, *L'Écume des jours*, in March 1947.

The prequel to *Vercoquin et le plancton*—*Trouble dans les andains* (literally, "Disorder in the Swaths")—had been written between 1942 and 1943, but would not be published until 1966, seven years after Vian's death. The two novels have often been dismissed as juvenilia. This may, in part, explain their never having been translated (in English, at least), though this could also be attributable to the dense punning and sophisticated cryptography of these early novels. No such barrier seems to have stood in the way of Vian's later works, however. Indeed, *L'Ecume des jours* has been translated three times.[6] Be that as it may, *Trouble dans les andains* (retrospectively) introduces the world to the stars of *Vercoquin et le plancton*, the double act that comprises the Major and Antioche Tambrétambre; it also makes use of techniques that would become—with some fine-tuning—defining features of Vian's novelistic output. As early as in 1970, Noël Arnaud put a positive spin on the question by suggesting that *all* Vian's work can be seen as juvenilia:

> All of Boris Vian's works are works of youth, of a wonderful youthfulness which has not stopped tickling the toes of mummies (in vain: mummies do not laugh, but it is good to imagine them laughing).[7]

The character of the Major takes the name of one of Vian's friends, Jacques Loustalot. Five years younger than Boris, the self-styled *bienheureux Major retour des Indes* ("joyful Major back from the Indies") had a glass eye, provocatively unconventional habits, and a penchant for partying. According to Arnaud, Vian was won over by the Major from their first encounter:

> He will become his inseparable friend, his double, his mirror, frequent house guest at Ville-d'Avray [the Vians' family home], and companion around Saint-Germain-des-Prés.[8]

Arnaud makes the additional point that *all* Vian's novels are *romans à cléf*— but having even a bunch of such keys matters little in terms of understanding the texts.[9] Nonetheless, it is tempting to read Vian's first two novels as homages to their friendship, not least because we might see aspects of Vian himself in the character of Antioche Tambrétambre.

As well as constituting an autobiographical celebration of young friendship, *Vercoquin et le plancton* can be read from many other angles. For example, in keeping with the surreal geometry governing Vian's literary world, parallel readings interweave and overlap—it is at once social documentary,[10] scathing satire, and jazz manifesto. Embroidered in the text are myriad references to French culture—embracing the novel, song, and poetry—and (sometimes painfully) cryptic plays on words: while the "joke" may often be styled as "adolescent" in nature, the technique is sophisticated, and the effect can be as disconcerting or disorienting as it can be amusing or offensive, depending on one's perspective. For Alain Costes, Vian's approach to language is "subversive." For Vian, he argues, words themselves—as well as conventional metaphors or sayings—are "stereotypes": Vian "subverts" language through the use of phonetic spelling and portmanteau words.[11] Olivier Bourderionnet has suggested that such techniques are akin to a "jazzy" style of writing. However, he argues, jazz was not merely "a prop" for Vian: it was a way of fusing the political and the poetic.[12]

In Occupied France, as Vian was writing *Vercoquin et le plancton*, the Zazous—of whom Vian was "undeniably perceived as a leader"[13]—had adopted musical tastes (American jazz and swing, banned by Nazi decree), fashions (extravagant clothing and hairstyles, at a time of rationing), and "habits" (at odds with the Vichy régime's "values"). With its detailed portrayal of Zazou style and antics, *Vercoquin et le plancton* can perhaps be seen in a vein of resistance or—as Sophie M. Roberts would put it—dissidence. Amid the craziness of Vian's portrayal, which is not unthinkingly uncritical of Zazous, it would be easy to forget what was at stake in "their symbolic rejection of Vichy through style."[14] Significantly, before and after their participation in the "yellow star campaign"—which saw young Swing fans wearing homemade yellow stars that sported words like "Swing" or "Zazou" instead of "Jew," many Zazous were arrested and sent to the French internment camps of Drancy and Tourelles.[15]

As Zazous morphed into beatniks, Vian would cause another national scandal in 1954 with a protest song decrying militarism: "Le Déserteur" ("The Deserter"). At a time of great colonial upheaval, the song itself was incendiary and was banned from broadcast. Beyond the lifting of the ban in 1962, this song has continued to resonate in Francophone cultures, with at least twenty-five cover versions spanning each decade to the present and— internationally—with translated recordings in at least eight languages.[16] Regarding his influence on music more generally, Vian has been hailed as the person who did more than anyone else to introduce the idiom, music, and aesthetic of jazz to France. Equally, he may be heralded—together with Henri Salvador—as the first French rocker.[17] Why stop there? It could be argued that Vian helped pave the way for punk. In her history of punk, whilst recognizing that neither "group" can be viewed as homogeneous, Caroline de Kergariou is not alone in seeing punks as kindred spirits—if not inheritors—of the Zazous:

> Appearing at the very beginning of the Second World War, the *zazous* are perhaps the closest thing that we can imagine to the spirit of provocative derision and derisory provocation that is the essence of punk.[18]

In this light, in its antiestablishment portrayal of convention-defying partygoers and youngsters who "do it themselves," *Vercoquin et le plancton*—and Vian—can certainly be assimilated into histories of subcultures and an overarching "philosophical tradition of cynicism" that does, indeed, include punk.[19]

DRAMATIS PERSONÆ

Focusing on the characters' names alone reveals the complexity of Vian's use of language; it also exposes some of the challenges in translating Vian. If Deleuze and Guattari had not developed their theory of the rhizome, it would have to have been invented to describe Vian's dense word association and polyphony:

> Semiotic chains of every nature are connected to very diverse modes of coding (biological, political, economic, etc.) that bring into play not only different regimes of signs but also states of things of differing status. . . . A rhizome ceaselessly establishes connections between semiotic chains, organizations of power, and circumstances relative to the arts, sciences, and social struggles. A semiotic chain is like a tuber agglomerating very diverse acts, not only linguistic, but also perceptive, mimetic, gestural, and cognitive: there is no language in itself, nor are there any linguistic universals, only a throng of dialects, slangs, and specialized languages.[20]

As a brief discussion of the characters' names will illustrate, Vian's wordplay can indeed be read as "coded": it associates—variously and simultaneously—the personal and the political, the natural world and the social world, the past and the present. Register ranges from the vulgar to the highly technical. Opening rhizomatic networks of association, rather than reflecting a hierarchy of meaning, the characters' names—like other forms of language play in Vian—are emblematic of polyphonic aspects of his writing.

For the most part, I have left the original characters' names intact. I generally rejected the option of anglicizing the more obscure names on the basis that "domesticating" them would detract from the atmosphere of the story. In other words, the story is set in France, so it is logical—and to be expected—that its French characters have French-sounding names.

However, as in many novelistic worlds, the very names of the characters are significant. For this reason, I have included lists of characters' names, including notes regarding their many possible and varied uses as signifiers—or rhizomatic nodes—in the novel.

The aim, in doing this, is not to limit interpretation or to reductively explain Vian's wordplay. Indeed, for Deleuze and Guattari, the rhizomatic could be seen as defying interpretation. The intention, therefore, is merely to facilitate entry into the text:

> It is perhaps characteristic of secret languages, slangs, jargons, professional languages, nursery rhymes, merchants' cries to stand out less for their lexical inventions or rhetorical figures than for the way in which they effect continuous variations of the common elements of language. They are chromatic languages, close to a musical notation. A secret language does not merely have a hidden cipher or code still operating by constants and forming a subsystem; *it places the public language's system of variables in a state of variation*.[21]

Often hidden or embedded, mixing slang with the technical, Vian's polyphony contains unlikely combinations of variables. The technique may be surrealist in design, humorous in effect, and the result can be dazzling. In this light, Ramiro Martín Hernández's exploratory study of onomastics in *Vercoquin et le plancton* comes to a beautiful conclusion: "Vian makes us participate in literary creation. The pleasure of the text becomes a reality for the part of the writer and for the part of the reader."[22] It is hoped that the following notes, written in this same spirit, provide relevant material useful in enabling this creative process and realizing that pleasure.

TRANSLATOR'S INTRODUCTION

MAIN CHARACTERS

Houspignole, Zizanie de la: *Zizania* is the genus of species of wild rice. The abstract noun *zizanie* is synonymous in French with "disorder," embracing trouble, conflict, if not chaos. It has the distinctive feature—unusual in French—of possessing two "z"s, in common with the words *zizi* (penis), *Zazou*, and *zozo* (a fool). I decided to leave this intact for a number of reasons: there is no ready or easy equivalent, it has the appearance of a French first name, and the "z"s of this Zazou's name point to her marginality.

The particle (*de la*) hints at aristocratic origins and, on one level, *Houspignole* could appear as a French equivalent of "Hispaniola." However, it potentially contains a less refined reference: the first meaning of the verb *se pignoler* (contracted and conjugated here as *s*[e] *pignole*) is "to masturbate."

Loustalot,[23] **Jacques (Le Major) / Jacques Lustalot (The Major):** In this character, Vian provides an affectionate portrait of his "inseparable" friend. The translation drops the "o" from the French, as the change is minor and the result can still pass as being French. It renders even more transparent—to an Anglophone audience—the novel's obsession with lust and all things sexual. His military title matches his civil status in this novel, as it starts with a party to celebrate his twenty-first birthday (or reaching the age of majority). His title also spurs wordplay—and even narrative—associated with the military (especially in Part IV). In the context of music—integral to Vian's work—the Major is a key:

> In general, it has been assumed by professional musicians and by interpreters of musical meaning that there is a difference in the affective qualities of the major and minor modes. The major is associated with the following characteristics: it is dynamic, an upward driving force; it is determining and defining, and more natural and

fundamental than the minor; it expresses varying degrees of joy and excitement; it sounds bright, clear, sweet, hopeful, strong, and happy.[24]

Tambrétambre, Antioche / Antioch Tambrétambre: Some critics have suggested that Vian portrayed something of himself in the figure of the Major's right-hand man. This certainly makes sense, given the obvious affection that Vian had for his friend. Perhaps unnecessarily, the translation anglicizes the original by dropping the "e" from the first name. The resultant equivalent is familiar if old-fashioned, and pronunciation is unambiguous. The surname, on the other hand, remains unchanged. More than just a touch of exoticism, retaining the acute accent allows readers with knowledge of French to pronounce his name (if only in their head) as the name is pronounced in French.

Antioch's surname has many musical associations, from timbre to tom-toms and tambours. It could also be a coded reference to the Tambour sisters, Germaine and Madeleine, who had links with Vian's stomping ground, the Hot Club de Paris; they were arrested by the German *Abwehr* in 1943.[25]

Vercoquin, Fromental de: The concrete noun *fromental* means "oat wheat." As an unusual, old-fashioned first name, it could call to mind the composer Fromental Halévy, most famous for his opera *La Juive* (The Jewess). Matching Zizanie's, his particle (*de*) again hints at aristocratic origins. The surname has been dissected in many ways. Some see in it a reference to the Maquis du Vercors (Free French Resistance group). Phonetically, the *ver-* conjures up "verse(s)," "glass(es)," "worm(s)," or even the adjectives "angry" and "green" (in the sense of inexperience). The adjective *coquin* might translate as "cheeky" or "saucy" (in the sense of kinky). As a noun, it denotes a rascal or a reprobate. Thus, any number of readings is possible by virtue of their permutation: for example, from "angry (or naïve) rascal(s)" to "kinky poem(s)."[26]

In the specialist field of neurodegenerative disorders, a *ver coquin* is responsible for causing the neurodegenerative disease scrapie in sheep. It is a lay term for a "prion," which can be defined as "A small, infectious pathogen containing protein."[27] Curiouser and curiouser is the fact that the word "prion"—in both French and English, however equally uncommon—is a polyseme with a separate meaning in the field of ornithology. The *Oxford English Dictionary* defines *prion* as "A small petrel of southern seas, having a wide bill fringed with comblike plates for feeding on planktonic crustaceans."[28] Such word association, learned and Loki-like mischievous to the point of impenetrability, at last reveals something approaching a logical link between "Vercoquin"—the character-cum-pathogen-cum-seabird—and the plankton of the novel's title.

OTHER

Leprince, Corneille: Lapprand informs us that this was the "affectionate nickname" for François Rostand, Vian's childhood friend and neighbor.[29] The novel is dedicated to his father, the biologist and philosopher Jean Rostand. At word level, we can note that a *corneille* is a crow (*Corvus*). In the history of French literature, Pierre Corneille was a seventeenth-century dramatist.

Marcadet-Balagny (Professor): Lapprand observes that this made-up professor owes his name to a Parisian Metro station which, in 1946, changed its name to commemorate Guy Môquet.[30] In 1941, Môquet was the youngest of some twenty-seven prisoners to be executed, and so "became the emblem of Communist engagement in the Resistance."[31]

LE CONSORTIUM NATIONAL DE L'UNIFICATION / NATIONAL CONSORTIUM FOR STANDARDIZATION

THE BOSSES

Baudrillon (Cardinal): For Lapprand, this name evokes that of Alfred Baudrillart (1858–1942): "A virulent anti-Bolshevik, this distant, austere man participated in the ambiguous relations between the Catholic church and the Nazi authorities throughout the Occupation."[32] Textually, *baudrillon* can be seen as a portmanteau, combining *baud* (a type of hunting dog) and *rillon(s)* (a dish made from pork belly fat).

Brignole, Joseph—Chief of Administration: Martín Hernández sees this surname as a portmanteau combining *brigue* ("craving") and *gnôle* ("hooch").[33]

Cercueil / Coffin—Head of Personnel: This surname is the French word for "coffin" or "casket."

Gallopin, Émile—General Chairman and Managing Director: The French noun *galopin* is frequently used condescendingly to refer to a rascal or scallywag.

Lavertu, Epaminondas—Head of the General Committee for Surprise Parties: In ancient Greece, the general and statesman Epaminondas (410–362 BCE) was known for his incorruptibility. Regarding the surname, literally meaning "virtue," Martín Hernández flags the irony that "Lavertu indulges in vice."[34]

Miqueut, Léon-Charles—Chief Junior Engineer: An equivalent for the surname might be "Halfcock." His name suggests that he is endowed with but a half-sized (*mi-*) penis (*queue*).

Requin—Central Government Delegate: Signifying "shark," this concrete noun has the same connotation of ruthlessness as in English.

Touchebœuf—Chief Engineer: A genuine family name of noble lineage, as a word it can be broken down to its constituent parts, *touche* and *bœuf*. A literal translation could be "bullock toucher." Martín Hernández points out that the "toucheur de bœufs"—according to the *Petit Robert* dictionary—is "responsible for moving his animals along by prodding them."[35]

Vautravers, André—Secretary General to the Delegation: In French, the compound prepositional form *au travers de* can translate as "by way of" or, more simply, as "through."

MIQUEUT'S DEPUTIES

Léger, Victor: In standard French, this surname variously signifies "light," "slight," "superficial," "fickle," or "unimportant." Ten men with the family name Léger are recorded as having been killed during the years 1942–1944.[36]

Levadoux, Henri: This surname—in the context of 1940s France—may have paid homage to Jean-Baptiste Levadoux, a member of the French Resistance who died on 19 July 1944 (*Maitron BDSGEM*). A more literary allusion lies in La Fontaine's ribald tale, "The Cordeliers of Catalonia." With the women of the town queuing at his door, one of the Cordeliers (Franciscan friars) advises them: "On en va mieux quand on *va doux*." In other words, they will have a better time if they "go softly," that is, take their turn on different days.

Marion, Jacques: Eight male Marions are recorded as having been shot, executed, or killed in action in 1943–1944 (*Maitron BDSGEM*). It can be noted that this character's surname is a Hebrew matronym. For his part, Martín Hernández draws attention to the fact that this name contains the word *mari* ("husband") and that the novel mentions his remarriage.[37]

Pigeon, Emmanuel: Neither of these names needs translating as such, but it is perhaps worth noting that Emmanuel is a Hebrew name, and that Pigeon has the additional connotation, in French, of "sucker" or "patsy." Once more, the name may simultaneously be a respectful nod to yet another member of the French Resistance who fell toward the end of the war: Fernand Pigeon was executed on 11 June 1944 (*Maitron BDSGEM*).

Troude, Adolphe: "Adolphe" used to be a common first name in the French-speaking world—see the inventor of the saxophone, Adolphe Sax, or the composer Adolphe Adam—but has, for obvious reasons, become very rare. "Troude" is a genuine family name, but it has comic potential in that it immediately evokes the expression *trou du cul* ("asshole").

Vidal, René: It could be a coincidence that a certain René Vidal was shot by German troops on 26 August 1944 (*Maitron BDSGEM*). Alongside this possibility, more textually, the name "René" literally means "reborn." The surname is composed, phonetically, of *vie* ("life") and *dalle* (a noun associated with hunger). It has been suggested that Vian portrayed something of himself in the character of Vidal. In a more autobiographical vein, indeed, the name "Vidal" is significant in relation to Vian's health. For Costes, it evokes Georges-Fernand Widal, the inventor of a diagnostic test for typhoid (which struck Vian at the age of fifteen). Costes also reiterates Arnaud's point that *le Vidal* is a long respected pharmaceutical dictionary in France.[38]

ADMINISTRATIVE STAFF
Alliage (Mademoiselle) / Miss Alliage—receptionist: The noun *alliage* is first and foremost a metallurgical term meaning "alloy." She is named for the first time in chapter XV, Part II. When she reappears in chapter III, Part IV, she has become Madame Legeai. As Martín Hernández has pointed out, *le geai* is the bird, the "jay."[39]

Balèze (Madame)—Miqueut's deputy secretary: In informal French, the adjective *balèze* means "huge" or "hefty."

TRANSLATOR'S INTRODUCTION

Cassegraine (Monsieur)—Office worker: This worker's name—mentioned only once in the novel—might be a reference to the French canning company Cassegrain, which continued production throughout the Occupation. More generally, a *casse-graine* is a "snack."

Lougre (Madame)—Miqueut's first secretary: There is something of the ogre (*l'ogre*) in this supposed family name.

Triquet (Madame)—administrative worker: This surname is homophonous with the French slang verb *triquer* ("to have an erection").

THE FINAL PARTY

THE BAND

Abadie, Claude: Born 16 January 1920, Abadie died in 2020. Vian played trumpet with Abadie's jazz orchestra—as does the character René Vidal—from 1942 to 1947.

D'Haudyt: This made-up surname is a convoluted transliteration of "Doddy," which was the nickname of Abadie's drummer, Claude Léon (1921–2000).

Gruyer, Jean: He played trombone with Abadie's band (dates unknown).

Hyanipouletos: According to Lapprand, this was the nickname of Jean Marcopoulos (1923–1953).[40] Known as Jean Marco, he sang and played guitar with Abadie and Vian. In the absence of this knowledge, it would be tempting to offer another hypothesis: "Hyanipouletos" presents as a torturous French transcription of "Johnny Puleo." Born in 1907, the diminutive Johnny Puleo is remembered as a harmonica-playing comedian and actor. He played with Borrah Minevitch's "Harmonica Rascals" in the 1930s and

'40s, and given that Minevitch is said to have moved to the suburbs of Paris in the mid-'40s,[41] it is quite possible that Vian was somehow familiar with this character and his comedic antics.

Lhuttaire: This is another transliteration, this time referring to Claude Luter (1923–2006), who played clarinet with Abadie's band in the 1940s and went on to form his own orchestra.

FRIENDS ET AL.

Duveau, Odilonne: The first name is the feminine form of "Odilon," which may call to mind Saint Odilon de Cluny, a medieval French Abbot. Her common surname literally means "From the calf/Some veal." In informal French, a *veau* is a "dunce."

Dumolard junior: While "Dumolard" is a perfectly unsurprising French family name, the noun *molard* translates to a "gob of spit."

Gna, Peter: According to Lapprand, this was the nickname of Vian's brother-in-law, Claude Léglise (1922–83).[42] Presenting as a very odd surname, "Gna" would be pronounced "nyah."

Métivier, Juste: The rue Juste-Métivier is in the 18th arrondissement of Paris, not too far from Montmartre Cemetery.

Planche, Berthe: As a cook, Berthe's surname—signifying, among other things, a board or platter on which food is served—may seem perfectly appropriate. However, her name can also be read as a Spoonerism: *pertes blanches* is a term in French meaning "vaginal discharge."

TRANSLATOR'S INTRODUCTION

Translating Vian is like trying to solve an avalanche of crossword clues. But there's a twist: the grid is four-dimensional, and the "clues" are hidden. Spoonerisms—especially in a name as banal as Berthe Planche—do not immediately jump off the page. Embedded "jokes," wordplay, and associations can pass unnoticed, even after several readings. For example, the narrator's summary of a rugby game between a team of road hauliers and a team of railway workers—*rugby route contre rugby rail* (chapter V, Part IV)—seems perfectly innocuous. Then—despite having read that phrase innumerable times—you realize that the prolific Boris has slipped yet another penis (via French slang, *biroute*) into his text. Because literal translation fails to capture either the sense or effect of this wordplay, I have sought creative solutions throughout.

Not content with punning in French, Vian seems to enjoy punning interlingually. In the made-up song titles, in particular, he has great fun in devising American-English titles that sound rude or otherwise humorous in French.[43] In addition, given the overt references in the novel to Indian customs and the Hindi language, it seems perfectly valid to credit Vian (or the Major) with having devised his famous (but—in French—meaningless) insult—*chichnoufs belouqués!*—through creative transliteration and Frenchification of the Hindi. The word "शशिन्" ("penis") sounds like "shishn," and "बेलोच" (pronounced "beloca") acts as the adjective "inelastic."

Aside from such linguistic virtuosity, the challenge of culture-specific idioms potentially pertains in any translation. However, in Vian's surrealist universe, the metaphorical can become "real," and this poses an extra challenge for the translator. For example, the "reality"—for the character Emmanuel—of "combing the giraffe," and its consequences, must necessarily be adapted to make sense in the context and logic of the story.[44] Then there's the plethora of cultural references. Many are musical, bringing Édith Piaf and Duke Ellington—among others—to the party. There are references—some more subtle than others—to literature, poetry, cinema, and theater: they mostly, but not exclusively, relate to the French cultural context. For example, the first lines of poetry that the Major recites to Fromental (chapter VIII, Part III) are a "pastiche" of poetry by José-Maria de Heredia.[45] This particular allusion—already obscure in the French context—is necessarily lost in translation. For the record, no attempt has been made in such cases to seek a cultural equivalent, as such "domestication" is tantamount to cultural imperialism. As Lawrence Venuti puts it, this strategy "reduc[es] if not simply exclud[es] the very difference that translation is called on to convey."[46]

More generally, Vian plays with historical, geographical, and geological references—as well as specialist terminology from fields as diverse as botany and mechanical engineering. In all these situations, I have sought to come up with creative solutions based on some form of wordplay or word association, in an attempt to mimic the polyphony of the original, even if the referents are different. A careful read of the names of the drinks listed in chapter II, Part I, should alert the reader to be on the lookout for such wordplay throughout the text, even in such superficially believable and exotic-sounding beverages as "Tunisian soukous," "L'Houpie juice," or "Van Audinayre wine."

To draw this introduction to a close, a word about political incorrectness. *Verocquin et le plancton* is not an anodyne novel. When it was written, it was deliberately and provocatively offensive. Today, it is offensive for different reasons. It is in the nature of stories to age—they age linguistically, as language itself evolves. They also age in that they reflect certain social and cultural attitudes, which also change over time—at least, that is, in terms of acceptability. Thus, while it was socially acceptable to publish *Tintin in the Congo* in 1932 with its racist language, attitudes, and representation of Black people, today that album has been boycotted, banned, or limited to restricted access. In *Vercoquin et le plancton*, we find only the odd reference to Black jazz musicians—but race is far from being a primary concern in this novel.[47] By modern standards, in the case of this novel, far more insensitive are certain of the narrator's comments on homosexuality and the representation of women.[48]

Whereas Monty Python were still able to joke about raping women in their 1979 film *The Life of Brian*, I should hope that today it has become a social taboo, more something to be outraged by than joked about. The same can be said for jibes about homosexuality. As Vian's novelistic intentions are impossible to define accurately, this translation seeks to tread the line between so-called fidelity—reproducing the violence and the relative cultural offensiveness of the original—and being sensitive and aware of the novel's new audience in the twenty-first century. That is not to say that this translation censors the original text, which has been translated *in extenso*. What it does mean, however, is that care has been taken to handle language sensitively in the original text relating to race, women, and homosexuality. My feeling (and justification) is that Boris Vian—were he among us, today— would not set out to offend in these ways. That said, I imagine the happily incorrigible Vian would have delighted in lampooning political correctness itself.

With thanks to Marc Lowenthal and Judy Feldmann, whose unstinting eye for detail has been inspiring.

For Ella.

NOTES

1. Some 484 of Vian's songs have been collected in Georges Unglik and Dominique Rabourdin, *Chansons—Boris Vian* (Paris: Christian Bourgois, 1984).

2. Ostensibly *translated*—rather than authored—by Vian from the work of the (nonexistent) Black American writer, Vernon Sullivan ("passing as white in life"), the novel's black protagonist passes "as white in the plot of the novel"

(Christopher L. Miller, *Impostors: Literary Hoaxes and Cultural Authenticity* [Chicago: University of Chicago Press, 2018], 82).

3. As a number of critics have suggested, the "popular" status of this novel should not be seen as a sign of poor quality (or gratuitous entertainment): "*J'irai cracher sur vos tombes* is an exercise in writing a bestseller that stages the writing of a bestseller in a preface and then again, *en abyme*, in its opening pages, only . . . at its conclusion to reveal itself to be the very antithesis of the model of bestseller-writing that it initially expounds" (Alistair Rolls, Marie-Laure Vuaille-Barcan, and Claire Sitbon, "*J'irai cracher sur vos tombes* and the *Série Noire*," *Francosphères* 5, no. 1 [2016]: 83).

4. Fabio Regattin explains that Vian would only admit authorship of this novel—in court—as late as November 1948. He goes on to affirm that Vian only narrowly escaped being sent to prison for writing this book, which would be banned in France from 1953 to 1973. See "Who Shall Spit on Your Grave? Quelques mots sur la traduction de 'J'rai cracher sur vos tombes (Boris Vian),'" *Synergies Inde* 6 (2013): 156.

5. *Œuvres romanesques complètes*, vol. 1 (Paris: Gallimard, 2010), 1138.

6. As *Froth on the Daydream*, trans. Stanley Chapman (London: Rapp & Carroll, 1967); *Mood Indigo*, trans. John Sturrock (New York: Grove Press, 1968); and *Foam of the Daze*, trans. Brian Harper (Los Angeles: TamTam Books, 2002). Stanley Chapman also translated *L'Arrache-cœur* (*Heartsnatcher* [London: Rapp & Carroll, 1968]). TamTam Books was also responsible for publishing Paul Knobloch's translations of *L'Automne à Pékin* (*Autumn in Peking* [Los Angeles: TamTam Books, 2005]), *L'Herbe rouge* (*Red Grass* [New York: TamTam Books, 2013]), and several of Vian's Vernon Sullivan novels.

7. Noël Arnaud, *Les Vies parallèles de Boris Vian* (Paris: UGE, 1970), 224. My translation.

8. Arnaud, *Les Vies parallèles*, 53.

9. Arnaud, *Les Vies parallèles*, 51.

10. To give just one example: "The word 'plankton' (used only twice in the prelude) must be taken metaphorically as designating the crumbs of a stolen loaf of bread, as opposed to the butcher's appetising red meat, an inaccessible luxury during the Occupation" (Marc Lapprand in Boris Vian, *Œuvres romanesques complètes*, vol. 1 [Paris: Gallimard, 2010], 1139).

11. Alain Costes, *Boris Vian: Le corps de l'écriture. Une lecture psychanalytique du désir d'écrire vianesque* (Limoges: Lambert-Lucas, 2009), 190.

12. Olivier Bourderionnet, "Jouer avec la forme: Politique et poétique du jazz dans la prose et les chansons de Boris Vian," *ATeM* 3, no. 2 (2018): 1–11.

TRANSLATOR'S INTRODUCTION

13. J. K. L. Scott, *From Dreams to Despair: An Integrated Reading of the Novels of Boris Vian* (Amsterdam: Rodopi, 1998).

14. Sophie B. Roberts, "A Case for Dissidence in Occupied Paris: The Zazous, Youth Dissidence, and the Yellow Star Campaign in Occupied Paris (1942)," *French History* 24, no. 1 (2010): 88.

15. Roberts, "A Case for Dissidence," 99.

16. Figures derived from https://secondhandsongs.com/work/56270/versions.

17. Kirk Anderson, "Song 'Adaptations' and the Globalisation of French Pop, 1960–1970," *French Cultural Studies* 26, no. 3 (2015): 333.

18. Caroline de Kergariou, *No Future: Une histoire du punk* (Paris: Perrin, 2017), 39.

19. De Kergariou, *No Future*, 39.

20. Gilles Deleuze and Félix Guattari, *A Thousand Plateaus: Capitalism and Schizophrenia*, trans. Brian Massumi (London: Continuum, 2003), 7.

21. Deleuze and Guattari, *A Thousand Plateaus*, 97.

22. Ramiro Martín Hernández, "Onomastique et jeu dans *Vercoquin et le plankton*," *Anuario de Estudios Filológicos* 9 (1986): 188.

23. In chapter XV of *Trouble dans les andains*, the narrator gives a long-winded explanation of the origins of this—his friend, the Major's—family name.

24. Kate Hevner, "The Affective Character of the Major and Minor Modes in Music," *American Journal of Psychology* 47, no. 1 (1935): 103–118.

25. Vian was still writing *Trouble dans les andains* and so in the process of creating Antioche at that time. For more on the Tambour sisters, see Rick Stroud, *Lonely Courage: The True Story of the SOE Heroines who Fought to Free Nazi-Occupied France* (London: Simon and Schuster, 2017), chapter 8.

26. From another angle, we can note that the noun *coq* ("rooster" or "cockerel") is embedded in the technical word *vérin* ("jack").

27. Michael P. McKinley and Stanley B. Prusiner, eds., *Prions: Novel Infectious Pathogens Causing Scrapie and Creutzfeldt-Jakob Disease* (San Diego: Academic Press, 1987), 42.

28. See: https://www.lexico.com/definition/prion.

29. *Œuvres romanesques complètes*, vol. 1, 1152.

30. *Œuvres romanesques complètes*, vol. 1, 1150.

31. Philippe-Jean Catinchi, "*L'Affaire Guy Môquet. Enquête sur une mystification officielle*, de Jean-Marc Berlière et Franck Liaigre: Malaise dans la commémoration," *Le Monde*, 3 November 2009.

32. *Œuvres romanesques complètes*, vol. 1, 1153.
33. Hernández, "Onomastique et jeu dans *Vercoquin et le plankton*," 185.
34. Hernández, "Onomastique et jeu dans *Vercoquin et le plankton*," 183.
35. Hernández, "Onomastique et jeu dans *Vercoquin et le plankton*," 186.
36. The *Maitron Biographical Dictionary of Those Shot, Guillotined, Executed, and Massacred* (1940–44) (*Maitron BDSGEM*) is exceptionally useful in providing this data. (For access to this information, and that regarding the names of the other deputies, see: https://fusilles-40-44.maitron.fr/.)
37. Hernández, "Onomastique et jeu dans *Vercoquin et le plankton*," 187.
38. Costes, *Boris Vian*, 203.
39. Hernández, "Onomastique et jeu dans *Vercoquin et le plankton*," 186.
40. *Œuvres romanesques complètes*, vol. 1, 1156.
41. Kim Field, *Harmonicas, Harps, and Heavy Breathers: The Evolution of the People's Instrument* (New York: Cooper Square Press, 2000), 53.
42. *Œuvres romanesques complètes*, vol. 1, 1156.
43. For this reason, I have not merely reproduced all of the English-language song titles of the original text. In some cases, they have been adapted with a view to achieving effects similar to those sparked by the original.
44. The uniquely French expression *peigner la girafe* (literally, "to comb the giraffe") is often translated as "to twiddle one's thumbs." As we might expect, ruder translations are available. See Chapter XVII, Part II.
45. *Œuvres romanesques complètes*, vol. 1, 1154.
46. Lawrence Venuti, *The Translator's Invisibility: A History of Translation*, 2nd ed. (New York: Routledge, 2008), 21.
47. Even so, and even as a vehement antiracist, Vian uses the word *nègre* (which I have translated as "Negro") in Part IV—socially acceptable in 1940s France, perhaps, but no longer.
48. In his psychoanalytical reading of Vian's texts, Costes suggests that—for Vian—"all women are sources of anxiety for man." This, he writes, is the "drama" of Vian's work (Costes, *Boris Vian*, 179).

VERCOQUIN AND THE PLANKTON

To Jean Rostand
with my apologies

PRELUDE

When you've spent your youth picking cigarette butts off the floor of the Deux-Magots, washing glasses in some dark and dingy back room, wrapping yourself in old newspapers in winter to keep warm on the frozen bench which is at once your boudoir, home, and bed; when you've been marched off by two gendarmes to the police station for stealing bread from the baker (having not yet learned that it's much easier to swipe it from the shopping bag of some old lady on her way back from market); when you've survived from one day to the next for three-hundred-and-sixty-five-and-a-quarter days a year, like the hummingbird in the branches of the hackberry tree; when, in short, you've fed on plankton, you have a rightful claim to the name of realist writer, and those reading your work will think to themselves: "This man has lived this story, he has experienced what he's portraying." They sometimes think other things, or nothing at all, but none of that's relevant to what follows.

I myself have always slept in a good bed, I don't like smoking, plankton is not at all to my taste, and if I were to steal anything, it would be meat. For butchers, innately fierier than bakers (who have as much fire in them as a steak tartare), won't send you off to a police station for trying to pilfer some crummy off-cut—which, moreover, bakers do not sell—but would much rather take it out on your body with a few good kicks to your gut.

Besides, this master work—by which I mean *Vercoquin et cætera*—is not a realist novel, in the sense that everything related herein really happened. Can the same truly be said for the novels of Emile Zola?

In this light, this preface is completely pointless and hence fulfills its intended function perfectly.

BORIS VIAN

PART I

Swing Time at the Major's

CHAPTER I

As he wanted to do things properly, the Major decided that his adventures would begin, this time, at the very moment he met Zizanie. The weather was splendid. The garden was brimming with newly hatched eglantines, the shells of which formed a crunchety carpet underfoot on the paths. Casting its dark shadow, a gigantic, tropical pie-scraper enshrouded the angle formed where the north and south walls of the sumptuous gardens surrounding the Major's residence—one of his many—converged. It was in this cozy atmosphere, that very morning, to the song of the Red *Disteda* crow, that Antioch Tambrétambre, the Major's right-hand man, had placed the green bench—made from the wood of the Indian cow crape jasmine tree—which was used on occasions such as these. And what was this occasion? Now is the time to say: it was February, in the middle of a heat wave, and the Major was going to be twenty-one years old. So he was throwing a party at his house in Ville-d'Avrille.

CHAPTER II

Complete responsibility for organizing the swinging shindig fell squarely on the shoulders of Antioch. He had much experience when it came to this sort of merriment, and the remarkable training he had put in over the years to consuming hectoliters of various fermented beverages with impunity singled him out as the best man, by a long chalk, for the job of getting everything ready for the party. For what Antioch had up his sleeve, the Major's house was perfect. He had planned it all down to a tee. He it was who had set up the record player with fourteen amps (including two acetylenal amps in case there was a power cut), which now formed the centerpiece of the Major's spacious lounge. The room was richly decorated with endocrine gland sculptures that Professor Marcadet-Balagny, the famous doctor at the Lycée Condorcet, would commission from the Special Police Detention Center specifically for the two hosts. Furniture-wise, all that remained in the vast room, which had been arranged especially for the grand occasion, were a number of luminescent narvik-skin sofas reflecting rosy hues from the rays of the sun, warming up nicely, and a couple of tables. The latter were overflowing with all sorts of treats, including saccharine pyramids, phonograph cylinders, ice cubes, Masonic triangles, magic squares, political spheres, ice-cream cones, a load of balls, etc. Bottles of Tunisian soukous rubbed shoulders with decanters of L'Houpie juice, New Comin-Steamin gin (from Dartmouth), Château Boques whisky, Van Audinayre wine, Thuringian vermouth, and such a variety of other exotic drinks that it was difficult to make them out. In front of the bottles, lenoxide crystal glasses laid out in serried rows stood waiting to receive the caustic cocktails that Antioch was readying himself to mix. The chandeliers were embellished with flowers whose penetrating scents were nearly enough to make one keel over, such was the power with which their unexpected fragrance punched. That was another of Antioch's touches. And then there were the records, piled high, shimmering with symmetrical, triangular reflections, waiting, quite impassively, for the moment when the needle of the record-player—ready to exfoliate them with its piercing caress—would wrench from their corkscrewing soul the cry it found suppressed within the dark groove.

The records that stood out in particular were *Song of the Booster* by Mildew Kennington and *Many Göer Gulls Down South* by Krüger and his Boers . . .

CHAPTER III

The Major's house was right next to the parc de Saint-Cloud, approximately two hundred yards away from the Ville d'Avrille train station, at 31 rue Pradier.

Standing in the shade of a 30 percent chemically pure wisteria plant, the majestic porch sheltered a flight of two steps which led to the Major's extensive lounge. The porch itself was reached by climbing twelve solid stone steps laid to interlock, ingeniously, in such a way as to form a stairway. From the gardens, covering some ten hectares (described in part in chapter 1), emanated a variety of scents, some of which, indeed, had a hint of currency. Day and night, wild rabbits roamed the fine lawns in search of earthworms, their favorite meal. Their long tails would trail behind them, producing the familiar crackling sound that many an explorer has heard and deemed perfectly innocuous.

A tame mackintosh, wearing a red leather collar with alabaster-white studs, was wandering full of melancholy down the garden paths, pining for the hills of his native land and the strains of the bagpipes that grew there.

The Sun cast his clear, liquid amber gaze over all things, and Mother Nature, full of midday joy, laughed with a toothy grin; three-quarters of her teeth had golden crowns.

CHAPTER IV

Given that the Major has not yet met Zizanie, his adventures have not started yet and, consequently, he cannot yet enter the stage. Thus, for the time being, we shall whisk ourselves away to the train station of Ville d'Avrille, at the precise moment when the Paris train came out of the dark tunnel fashioned in such a way as to protect a section of the railway linking Ville d'Avrille to Saint-Cloud.

Before the train had come to a complete standstill, a tight crowd began to trickle through the automatic doors that were the pride and joy of Parisians using Saint-Lazare train station—despite having had nothing at all to do with their invention—until, that is, the introduction of the so-called oxidizable wagons on the Montparnasse lines that combine automatic doors *and* steps that extend (or contract, willy-nilly), which is no mean feat.

The tight crowd began to flow fitfully to the one and only exit gate, guarded by the ginger-haired guard, Pustoc. The tight crowd was made up of numerous youngsters of both sexes, and such was the extent to which they exhibited a total lack of personality and acted so freely that the man at the gate said: "To get to the Major's place, go over the walkway, carry on up the road opposite the station, take the first right, and then the first on the left, and you're there." "Thanks," said the young men, whose suits were very long and whose companions were very blonde. In total, there were about thirty of them. More would arrive by the next train. More would arrive by car. All were going to the Major's.

They headed up avenue Gambetta, walking slowly, and bellowed as Parisians do when in the countryside. When they saw a lilac tree, they exclaimed: "Look! A lilac tree." It was pointless. But it showed the girls that they knew a thing or two about botany.

They reached 31 rue Pradier. Antioch had thought to leave the gate open. They entered the Major's pretty gardens. The Major was not there yet, because Zizanie was due to arrive by car. The youngsters taunted the mackintosh, who responded with a "Pssh" and walked off. They then climbed the porch steps and went into the lounge. Thereupon, Antioch unleashed the head-spinning harmonies of the record-player and the so-called surprise party began.

At that precise moment, a car growled at the gate, entered the gardens, followed the track to the left, skidded in order to pull up in front of the porch, stopped and then carried on skidding because the driver had forgotten to brake, turned round, stopped in front of the porch, and stayed stopped.

A young woman got out of the car. It was Zizanie de la Houspignole. Behind her came Fromental de Vercoquin.

There was complete silence and then the Major appeared at the top of the steps.

"Hello," he said, visibly shaken.

CHAPTER II

(It's only chapter 11 because the Major's adventures began in the preceding chapter with the arrival of Zizanie.)

So, shaken, the Major walked down a few steps, shook hands with the two new guests and showed them into the spacious lounge awash with couples jerking to the sound of "Keep my Wife until I Come Back to My Old Country Home in the Beautiful Pines (Down the Mississippi River that Runs across the Screen with Ida Lupino)," which was all the rage. It was a drawn-out eleven-bar blues number to which the songwriter, with some skill, had added elements of swing-waltz. It was a perfect record with which to kick off a party: not too slow and quite rousing, it made enough noise to be heard above the excited voices and dancing feet.

The Major, abruptly ignoring Fromental's presence, took Zizanie by the waist with both hands and said to her: "Will you dance with me?" "Certainly . . ." she replied. Dexterously, he slid his right hand toward her neck; with his left hand, more sinister, he squeezed her fingers, now resting on his muscular shoulder.

The Major danced in a rather unique manner; at first sight, it could be a little unnerving, but one soon got used to it. At various intervals, having planted his right foot, he would raise the left leg in such a way that the femur made a right angle with the upright body. The tibia, held parallel to the body, would then flick out slightly, as if in spasm, but the foot would remain perfectly horizontal throughout. When the tibia returned to a vertical position, the Major would lower his femur and carry on as if nothing had happened. He avoided making big steps, which are tiring, and always stayed roughly in the same place, with a great big grin on his face.

Meanwhile, his active mind came up with an original opening gambit.

"Do you like dancing, mademoiselle? . . ."

"Yes, indeed," Zizanie replied.

"And do you dance often? . . ."

"Erm . . . Yes," Zizanie replied.

"What's your favorite? . . . Swing?"

"Oh, yes," Zizanie replied.

"Have you been dancing swing long?"

"Why . . . Yes," Zizanie replied, astonished.

The question, as far as she was concerned, was redundant.

"Please don't think for a second that I ask you that because I believe you dance badly. Nothing could be further from the truth," the Major added. "You dance like someone who's used to dancing often. But it could be that you're simply gifted and maybe you've only been dancing for a short time . . ."

He gave a silly laugh. Zizanie laughed too.

"So," he continued, "you dance often?"

"Yes," Zizanie replied with conviction.

The record stopped playing at this point and Antioch went over to the record player to keep people from meddling with it. It was an automatic, so there was no need for anyone to start touching it. However, a certain Janine—known to be a danger when records were around—was hovering, and Antioch wanted to avoid any complications.

Meanwhile, the Major said, "Thank you, young lady," but didn't move. Whereupon, Zizanie said, "Thank you, Monsieur," and gently extricated herself, glancing around the room in search of someone. That was Fromental de Vercoquin's cue to sweep in and usher Zizanie away. Instantaneously, there rang out the first bars of "Until My Green Rabbit Eats His Soup like a Gentleman," and the Major felt his heart pierced, stung by the stylet of a flea trapped between his shirt and his skin.

Despite appearances and despite having brought her to the party, Fromental didn't know Zizanie very well, having met her for the first time just a week earlier at the house of some mutual friends; he took it upon himself to make conversation with her during this next dance.

"You've never come to the Major's before?"

"Oh, no," replied Zizanie.

"There's never a dull moment," said Fromental.

"No . . ." replied Zizanie.

"You've never seen the Major before?"

"Why, no," said Zizanie.

"Do you remember the guy we saw last week, when we were at the Popeyes? The tall guy, with light-brown, wavy hair . . . You know who I mean? He's a regular . . . You get me?"

"No . . ." said Zizanie.

"You don't like waltzes, do you?" he said, to change the subject.

"No," said Zizanie with conviction.

"Please don't think," said Fromental, "that I ask you that because I think you dance swing badly. Quite the opposite. I think you're a great dancer. The way you follow is . . . it's *perfect*. I'd swear you'd been taught by professionals."

"No . . ." replied Zizanie.

"So, you've not been dancing long, then?"

"No . . ." replied Zizanie.

"That's a shame . . ." Fromental went on. "And yet your parents don't mind you going out?"

"No," replied Zizanie.

Their dance ended when the record stopped. It had lasted a little longer than the one with the Major because when the latter had exerted his gravitational pull, the preceding tune had already begun.

Fromental said:

"Thank you, young lady," and Zizanie said:

"Thank you, Monsieur." Antioch, who was walking past and whose manner was generally relaxed, quite informally wrapped his arm round the damsel's waist and whisked her to the bar.

"Your name's Zizanie?" he asked.

"Yes. What's yours?"

"Antioch," replied Antioch, whose name, indeed, was undeniably Antioch.

"That's a funny name, Antioch ... So! Antioch, pour me a drink."

"What would you like to drink?" asked Antioch. "Some vitriol or cyanide?"

"A bit of both," replied Zizanie. "I'll leave it up to you."

The Major watched Antioch somberly as the preliminary arpeggios of the third record—"Toddlin' with Some Skeletons"—rang out.

"What do you think of the Major?" asked Antioch.

"Very nice ..." replied Zizanie.

"And your friend, Fromental," said Antioch, "what does he do?"

"I don't know," said Zizanie. "He's an idiot. He doesn't know how to have a conversation. But he's been boring me stiff for a week now on the basis that his family knows my family."

"Oh?" said Antioch. "Here ... Get that down you, my blonde beauty. And don't worry—there's more where that came from."

"Really?"

She drank. Her eyes began to gleam.

"It tastes really good ... You're definitely a man who's up to the job."

"You bet!" agreed Antioch, who was six feet tall—not an inch less—and had all his teeth.

"Will you dance with me?" asked Zizanie, coquettishly.

Antioch, who had noticed the practical design of her dress, with its corsage made up of a loose fabric crossing over the breasts and then wrapped about the midriff, led her to the middle of the room.

The Major was dancing absentmindedly with a large brunette who had noticeably smelly armpits and danced with her legs apart. Probably to dry off.

Antioch opened the conversation.

"Have you ever thought," he asked, "how practical it is to own a driving license?"

"Indeed," said Zizanie. "In fact, I got mine two weeks ago."

"Aha!" said Antioch. "When will you give me lessons?"

"Well . . . whenever you want, my friend."

"And what is your honest opinion of snails?"

"They're great!" she said. "When they've got smoke in their eyes."

"So, you'll give me a lesson next week," said Antioch.

"Don't you have a driving license?" asked Zizanie.

"Of course I do! What's that got to do with it?"

"Now you're teasing me, you are."

"I should allow no such thing, my dear," said Antioch.

He held her slightly closer to his body and, all in all, she did not seem to mind. However, Antioch quickly let go of her when he realized that she was going to put her cheek against his, and he had the distinct impression that his underpants would not bear the strain.

Once more the music stopped, and Antioch managed to save appearances by discreetly slipping his right hand into his trouser pocket. Taking advantage of the fact that Zizanie had spotted a friend, he joined the Major in a corner of the room.

"You swine!" said the Major. "You're stealing her from me!..."

"She's not ugly!..." replied Antioch. "You had designs on her?"

"I love her!" said the Major.

CHAPTER III

Antioch seemed pensive.

"Listen," he said. "I've no intention of letting you do anything foolish. Let me look after her for a while, and then I'll let you know if she's the one for you."

"You really are a good friend," said the Major.

CHAPTER IV

The party had got off to a good start. That was only to be expected when all the guests arrive at roughly the same time. Generally, when they don't, you have to put up with boring weirdos for the first couple of hours, as they're always the first to turn up, with their homemade cakes which look terrible but taste great, nonetheless.

The Major did not like such cakes and so his parties tended to be rigged, as it were, in the sense that he provided both drink and food. That way, he enjoyed relative independence as far as his guests were concerned.

DIGRESSION

It's quite depressing to find oneself accidentally at a party that gets off to a bad start.

The host—or hostess—of the house sits in the empty room, with two or three friends who have arrived early, without even a pretty girl for company. Because pretty girls always arrive late.

This is when the younger brother will share risqué displays he won't dare share later on. Not least because he will have been locked up.

All you can do is watch the two or three unfortunates adopt pleasing poses in the parlor with the freshly waxed parquet floor, imitating such-and-such or so-and-so—the difference being that the latter know how to dance properly.

They too won't dare, later on . . .

Now, imagine you've arrived later than them at this party. When the party is in full swing.

You enter the room. Good frenz slap you on the back. Those you have no desire to shake hands with are already on the dance floor—they dance constantly, which is why you never quite see eye to eye with them—and with a solitary glance you check to see if there are any girls available. (A girl is available if she's pretty.) If there are, everything's fine: it's still the start of the party and they've been neither invited to dance too much nor worked upon to any dangerous level, because the boys who have turned up alone—mostly due to being shy—haven't yet had enough to drink as to be so bold.

You, however, have no need to drink to be so bold and you also always arrive on your own.

Don't try to be witty. They never understand. And those that do understand are already married.

Get her to have a drink with you. That's it.

Now you have the opportunity to activate your prodigious cunning in finding a bottle of something to drink.

(You simply take it from the secret hiding place you've just shared with some newly arrived guest who's not quite with it.)

Hide it in your trousers. Allow only the bottleneck to protrude above your belt. Approach your prey once more. Assume a benign countenance, laced with a hint of mystery. Take her by the arm, or the waist even, and whisper: "It's up to you to find a glass—one will be enough for the pair of us. I've held my end of the bargain . . . Shush . . ."

Then you sneak into the bedroom next door. Does it lock? Hey! What a surprise. Inside the room is the Admiral. He's a friend. Of course, he's not alone. You knock on the door, either three quiet knocks and a loud one, or seven medium knocks and two quiet ones, depending on what was agreed with the Admiral. As soon as you've been let in, quickly lock the door and don't stare too much at the Admiral, who'll be returning to the line of battle. He'll leave you to your own devices, immersed in the delicate operation of trying to slide his hand into the skirt of his partner, an intelligent young woman, intelligently dressed. Now pull out your bottle, which is a little chilly, but without taking stuperfluous precautions, because the Admiral has his own. Stay close to the door, ready to hear her knock when she comes back . . .

And she doesn't come back . . .

To help you get over this shock, open the bottle. Take a good swig. Careful! Drink no more than half the bottle! Hope may be at hand . . .

Knock, knock! Someone's at the door . . .

YOU (*in a severe tone, by way of reprimand*): Couldn't you have got back a bit quicker?

HER (*feigning surprise but satisfied*): You're mean!

YOU (*gently pulling her to you by the waist*): I'm not mean . . . And you know it . . .

HER (*pretending to pull away, giving you the chance to examine her right breast*): Hey, hey, be a good boy . . .

YOU (*still examining her right breast, whilst ostensibly contemplating something entirely different, and in a very relaxed manner*): Did you find a glass?

HER (*triumphantly pulling out a thimble*): Why, of course! Ta-da!

(*She continues.*) Jacques invited me for a dance, you see, and I couldn't say no . . .

YOU (*grumpily*): Who's this Jacques guy?

HER: Jacques! He's the one who brought me here in his car!

YOU: Oh, the cretin with the dirty blond hair?

HER: Actually, he's very kind. And he doesn't have dirty blond hair . . .

YOU: So, you like dirty blond hair . . .

HER (*coquettish, laughing*): Why, of course!

YOU (*angry, because you have brown hair*): There's no accounting for taste . . .

HER: Don't be silly . . .

(*She laughs and comes slightly closer to you, placing her right hand on your left biceps, her arm bent. You put your right arm around her, gently squeeze, and say:*)

"You're not drinking?"

"You've not given me anything to drink."

So, you pour with your free left hand, you drink together, and you spill most of yours down your tie. You haven't a handkerchief. Feeling fed up you sit down on the only free seat (in view of the fact that the Admiral is taking up almost the entire sofa). Standing in front of you, she wipes your tie with her handkerchief.

"It's easier like this, you're so tall . . ."

She turns a little, with her left side facing you, and all it takes is the slightest of prods to make her fall onto your right knee.

What happens next depends on your fancy at the time.

Afterward, she gives you a striking description of the type of boys she likes, but only after checking your eyes so as to avoid saying brown if yours are blue.

This is what happens at these parties when you're not put off, in the first instance, by the truly bizarre faces of the few women available.

In cases where you are put off, the required technique is a lot more complicated.

Note:

The parties discussed here are those decent parties where guests fornicate in separate couples, and only do so in rooms cut off from the dancing room, if only by means of a curtain.

Other parties are a lot less interesting and never yield the results one can achieve by contacting the professionals of this type of sport.

CHAPTER V

The Major had, in his youth, studied the theoretical solution to the problem described at the end of the final paragraph of the digression above.

Two variants may be encountered:

A) *THERE ARE NO PRETTY GIRLS WHATSOEVER.*
This is a relatively frequent eventuality, especially if you're a bit picky.
  a) *The surprise party is well organized.*
     Make do with the buffet, that's all there is to it. This situation, indeed, will only arise if you're at someone else's party, because you only organize parties at your house if you're certain that pretty girls will be there, so there's no reason to have any qualms about tucking into the buffet at someone else's house if they can't even be bothered to provide this vitally important delicacy for you.
  b) *The party is badly organized.*
     Leave at once and try to take some item of furniture with you by way of recompense.

B) *THERE ARE PRETTY GIRLS AT THE PARTY, BUT THEY ARE TAKEN.*
This is where the fun begins.
  a) *You work alone (as a lone wolf).*
     I. *IN YOUR OWN HOME.*
        Do what it takes to rid yourself of the troublesome individual using a variety of means in line with the intrinsic nature of that individual, while forcing yourself to stay with him for as long as possible.
        Working alone, pretty much the only means available to you involves getting him to drink, while taking care:
          a) to prevent his partner, whom you covet, from drinking too much or too close to him;
          b) not to drink as much as he does.

Ply him with mixtures of drinks from leftover glasses that would make a Senegalese man turn salmon pink. As soon as his vision starts to blur, color the cocktails with dark port and add cigarette ash. Take him away to vomit:

a) to a sink, if he has only been drinking;
b) to the toilet, if he has been eating cake, because bits of apple would block the sink;
c) outside, if you have a garden and it's raining.

Make sure his partner comes with you. There's a chance she'll be put off by all this. Whatever you do, ensure that he covers himself with opprobrium. Then lay him down in a safe place.

Two further variations can, in this situation, arise:

a) his partner lets him sleep.

In this case, you've won. If he's been given the job of escorting her home, sober him up, when it's convenient to do so, by vigorously wiping his face with a dirty dish-cloth or by getting him to drink a glass of Eno's fruit salts or a *café au vitriol* (but go easy on the vitriol).

b) she remains stubbornly devoted and stays with him.

It is highly likely that they're engaged. There's still a chance you might see them shagging,* if you come back without making any noise an hour later. It's good for a bit of fun if you have a maid who cleans for you.

The case of the parasite: there is no way of sobering the guy up.

....

* Hexcuse me, but that's what it's called.

There is no way round this, unless you're much, much stronger than he is.

2. *IN SOMEONE ELSE'S HOME.*

a) *At the house of an individual whose partner you covet.* He is in a very strong position, because it's quite unlikely that he'll get dead drunk.

Try to take him out of the equation by using one of the following methods:

1) Cause a deliberate flood in his bathroom:
   a) using part of an inner tube from a bicycle tire (make sure you bring this with you);
   b) using a bit of rubber tubing (found on a gas heater or stove, but often too small);
   c) by wedging a toothbrush tumbler under one of the bath taps (a method at once simple, elegant, and efficient).

2) Block the evacuation pipe using two rolled-up news-papers (yields excellent results).

3) Get one of the host's good friends dead drunk, using the methods given above. The host does, however, risk returning to recover his property as soon as you start working on it. His property, moreover, may well have no desire whatsoever to change pony, because the host is the one with the keys to the bedrooms. Or perhaps because he's as competent as you?

b) *At the house of a complete stranger.*

In this scenario, you are roughly on an equal foot-ing. In other words, the odds are pretty much against you. Even so, try to get him smashed. No mean feat if you have no booze on you (hence the potential outlay), but if you do provide drink he might become so buddy-buddy with you and be so moving in his outpourings regarding your plan that he breaks your heart. If that happens, all that will remain for you to do is give the love birds your blessing. There is no escape, sometimes, from one's innate humanity.

Consequently, working alone makes this no easy feat.

b) *You are working as part of a team.*
It matters little, in this scenario, whether you are at home or at the home of some Tom, Dick, or Harry. It is an extremely simple job and you need no more than a team of four, yourself included, to yield excellent results. The main risk in this strategy involves seeing one of your teammates appropriate the prize of the operation for himself. Don't lose sight of this when choosing your teammates. The all-too-easy strategy of getting the mark drunk—reserved for those cases described above—is, in this instance, out of the question. If it is mentioned, here, it is by way of counterexample, included to exemplify the holistic nature of this study.

PRINCIPLE—Make your enemy disappear:
1) Under a thick cloak of shame, using one of the following means:
a) Goad him into picking a fight with the skinny guy (one of the four) in the background who looks like a weakling, wears glasses, and has been practicing judo for the last six years.

The other two can finish him off with hefty glasses of firewater by way of consolation;

b) Get him to play some silly game involving strip-
ping (and cheat, of course). This is not advisable
if he is better at cheating than you are (in any case,
wear clean underwear and socks), nor if he turns
out, when naked, to be rippling with muscle on
muscle ... In short, remember that he might well
remain clothed whereas you might not, so follow
your instincts but be modest.

> This strategy is worth trying if he is wearing
sock suspenders and long johns.

2) By putting him out of circulation.

> This procedure—undertaken in the correct
manner—can only result in:

a) the patient being transported to the cellar or to
the toilet;

b) his departure, with you at his side (in a friend's
car). You get him to drink lots of beer in the local
bar and you leave him pissing against a tree seven
miles from the house. Alternatively, suggest a
swim in the river, in the middle of nowhere, and
completely destroy his trousers. There are many
variations on this;

c) *the pièce de résistance* ... he is left in the hands of
an operator, fully qualified and open-minded.

NOTA BENNY: THIS RESEARCH LOSES MUCH OF ITS INTEREST IF
YOU PREFER BOYS. IN THIS CASE, WE STRONGLY RECOMMEND
YOU CONSULT THE RENOWNED WORK OF GENERAL PIERRE
WEISS: *A SHOT IN THE DARK*.

BORIS VIAN

CHAPTER VI

This essential digression has made it clear that the Major's jamborees were not surprise parties in any coarse way and, therefore, that the preceding parenthesis has no bearing whatsoever on the adventure yet to befall the Major.

CHAPTER IV

As revealed in chapter VI, chapters IV and V are only tangential to the Major's story, so it would seem wise to return to chapter IV.

Having said, "You really are a good friend," the Major planted an affectionate kiss on Antioch's forehead, the latter having bowed slightly, and then he went off to his gardens in search of his mackintosh because he didn't want to get in the way of Antioch's efforts.

The mackintosh, sitting at the foot of a Madagascan spruce, was whimpering pitifully. The hullaballoo of the party was not at all to his liking and his claws were hurting him.

"You're bored, aren't you?" kindly enquired the Major, stroking the mackintosh between his hind quarters.

The mackintosh discharged a few drops of some fetid fluid and fled with a "Psssh!"

Now alone, the Major surrendered to thoughts about his love life.

He picked a China aster, carefully counted the number of petals, to be sure there was no risk, and, having reckoned their sum to be a multiple of five minus one, began picking them off.

"She loves me . . ." he sighed,

"A little
    A lot
        Passionately
            Madly
                Not

A little
    A lot
        Passionately
            Madly
                Not

A little
    A lot
        Passionately
            Madly
                Not..."

"Shit!" he cried.
Of course, he had missed one.

CHAPTER V

"She can't love me yet," pondered the Major, to console himself, "because she doesn't know me well enough..."

Yet the very restraint of this thought did nothing at all to console him.

He shot up the path and found Fromental's car. It was a Debrieka in competent red, with a wide chrome band around the fuel tank cap. It was, of course, the latest model, with twelve cylinders arranged as hemistichs in V-formation. Like Verlaine, the Major preferred odd numbers.

Suddenly, Fromental de Vercoquin appeared on the porch, and he was dancing with Zizanie. The Major's heart went "Splosh" in his chest and stopped beating altogether, wrong side up. At least, that is how it felt to the Major.

He watched the two of them closely. The record stopped. It was "Give Me That Bee in Your Trousers." Immediately, another tune began: it was "Holy Pooh Doodle-Dum Dee-Do," and Antioch appeared on the steps and asked Zizanie to dance. To the Major's great relief, she accepted, and his heart started beating again.

Now alone on the porch, Vercoquin lit a cigarette and started to casually descend the steps.

He walked up to the Major who was still looking at the Debrieka, and, feeling very well disposed to him, said enthusiastically:

"How about a ride? Want to try it?"

"Gladly," said the Major with a benevolent grin, a mask of apparent kindness veiling an underworld of Miltonian pandemonium.

A fifth of a mile away from the Major's place, at the end of avenue Gambetta, Fromental followed the Major's directions to turn right. At the Ville d'Avrille church, he turned left onto the tarmacadam road leading to Versailles.

At Old Otto's restaurant, the Major gestured to Vercoquin to pull over.

"Let's go for a drink," he said. "The beer here is top-notch."

They leaned on the bar.

The Major gave the order: "A pint for my friend, and I'll have a port!"

"You're not having a beer?" asked Vercoquin, surprised.

"No," said the Major. "It plays havoc with my joints."

This was a complete lie. The only effect that beer had ever produced in the Major was a rapid but fleeting swelling of the lower extremities.

Vercoquin drank his pint.

"Another!" the Major ordered.

"But . . ." Fromental protested, burping noisily.

"Pish . . . Pardon," said the Major. "Granted . . . Think nothing of it."

Vercoquin drank his second pint, the Major paid for the rounds, and then they left, got back in the Debrieka, and set off for Versailles.

They went through that old town still reeking of the Great King's pong, powerful and distinctive, and carried on up to the forest of Marly.

"The car runs like a dream," the Major said, politely.

"*Oui*," replied Fromental. "But I do need to take need a piss . . . "

CHAPTER VI

The Major, at the wheel of the superb Debrieka in competent red, sped up the track through his gardens, and came to a halt in front of his steps with no mean mastery. The car rolled back, but he had already got out, and the Debrieka crashed into the wall next to the gate, damaging only a Chinese lacquer tree not quite dried and which got slightly scratched.

The Major was greeted by Antioch at the top of the steps.

"He didn't read chapter v . . ." intoned the Major.

"Well, he doesn't count," replied Antioch.

"True," said the Major. "Poor guy!"

"You're too compassionate," asserted Antioch.

"True," said the Major. "What a beastly person he is! What an inexorable cretin!" (The Major did not put undue stress on the "ex" of "inexorable.")

"Quite right," agreed Antioch.

"What about Zizanie?" asked the Major.

"She's gone to spruce herself up."

"When was that?"

"Fifteen minutes ago. It wasn't easy finding her a needle and thread," Antioch continued.

"What sort of thread?" the Major enquired discreetly, obliquely.

"The same color as her knickers," replied Antioch, equally discreetly.

"Did you give her a strong thread?" asked the Major, somewhat worried.

"Yeah, right," said Antioch. "I gave her rayon. It comes apart when wet."

CHAPTER VII

In the Major's spacious lounge, the party had reached its high point. The lord of the manor went in, followed by Antioch, and went straight to the bar, as his throat was as dry as an agricultural committee coat hanger.

He poured himself a fizzy orange, drank, and spat out a pirrip pip that had found its way under his tongue. Antioch was mixing himself an extra-special Monkey Gland. It was hot. It was good. It smelt like a duffel bag should (as Édith Piaf—whose take on odor vies with the depraved—would say).

Having finished his drink, Antioch slid behind Zizanie who was conversing merrily, as the old saying goes, with a friend. Her friend's not bad either, thought the Major, who—allowing his accomplice to carry out the screen test—was looking for an ersatz soulmate.

Having slid behind Zizanie, Antioch grabbed her by the thorax with both hands, quite gently and very naturally, and planting a kiss on the left side of her temple, asked her to dance.

She excused herself and followed him to the middle of the room. He embraced her tightly in order to hide, behind the young blonde's Scots pleated skirt, that part of his profile between his belt and his knees. Then he got into the rhythm of "Cham, Jonah, and Joe Louis Playing Monopoly Tonight," the harmonies of which rose and rose, imperiously.

The Major moved in on Zizanie's friend, whom he bored to death by interrogating her for the duration of six dances about Zizanie's background: what she liked doing, how often she went out, her childhood, and so on and on.

Meanwhile, the gate bell tinkled and the Major, having reached the front door, made out the distant silhouette of one of his neighbors, Corneille Leprince, whom he had not forgotten to invite. His property was twenty yards from the Major's, and Corneille was always the last one to arrive because, what with living so nearby, he never needed to hurry to be on time. Hence his lateness.

CHAPTER VIII

Corneille had been suffering a periodic beard that grew at a speed equaled only by that with which he had unexpectedly decided, after keeping it for six months, to begrudgingly rid himself of it.

Corneille was wearing a navy-blue suit, outrageously pointy yellow shoes, and very long hair he had taken care to wash the day before.

Corneille was a man of many talents: the medieval virelay, palm-racquetball, pong ping, mathematics, manky-tonk piano, and a host of other hobbies that he couldn't be bothered with. Yet he did not like dogs, or pneumonia, or any monia of any age or any of the illnesses to which he succumbed with revolting ease.

One thing he hated in particular was the Major's mackintosh.

He came across the thing where the path curved and shied away from it in revulsion.

Incensed, the mackintosh went "Psssh!" and left.

Apart from that, girls generally agreed that Corneille would have been a charming boy had he regularly shaved his beard, with a week's notice, reduced the extent of his luxurious bush, and looked less as if he had been rolling around in crap every time he wore the same suit for more than two days running.

Good old Corneille genuinely cared very little about personal hygiene.

Corneille eventually made it into the Major's house and they shook hands in their own ritualistic manner: thumb against thumb, index pulling index, with each of these digits forming a hook perpendicular to its respective thumb, and with both hands being raised at the same time at an even pace.

He shook hands in this same way with Antioch, who said:

"So, Corneille, you made it! How's your beard?"

"I shaved it off this morning!" said Corneille. "And it looks awful."

"Is it because of Janine?" asked Antioch.

"Of course it is," said Corneille, gnashing his teeth. It was sort of how he smiled.

With no further ado, Corneille made a beeline for Janine, who was just about to get her mitts on "Palookas in the Milk," one of Bobby Crossbow's latest records that Antioch had only recently acquired. She didn't see him coming and Corneille, holding out his index finger, pushed it quite callously into the flesh of her right shoulder. She started and without a word began dancing with him, the air thick with tension. She was sorry about the record.

Every now and then, he leaned backward, with a turn and a spin, as it were, on his heels, such that his body would fall to an angle of seventy-five degrees to the horizontal. At the point of falling over, he would catch himself, through some sort of miracle, by suddenly changing direction with the pointy ends of his shoes unfailingly pointed upward and his partner held at a respectful distance. He almost never went forward, preferring rather to pull on his partner like an emergency lamppost he could hang on to. Not a second went by without his laying out some unwary couple onto the floor, and after ten minutes of this, the middle of the room was indisputably his.

When he was not busy dancing, Leprince would imitate the cry of the chonchon bird or get stuck into drinking a fraction approaching an eleventh of a glass of diluted alcohol, so as not to get too tipsy too quickly.

The Major was still dancing with Zizanie's friend, and Antioch had just disappeared into the private little shaggoir just off the dancing room, where he found piles and piles of coats.

Accompanied, of course, by Zizanie.

CHAPTER IX

As the merriment of the partygoers seemed to him to be waning, a tall guy with ginger hair who lisped badly, despite bearing the eminently American name of Willy or Billy, depending on when you asked him, took it upon himself to spread some joy.

He stopped the record player with devilish skill by pulling the plug out—a neat trick that Antioch had overlooked—and plonked himself in the middle of the room.

"And now," he said, "I invite each and every one of you, just to mix things up a little, to tell a joke or two . . . or sing a song. I don't want to seem like a chicken, so I'll go first."

His lisp was so bad that it was necessary, when listening to him, to adjust one's orthography.

"Here'f a funny ftory for you," he said. "It'f about a man who hath trouble pronounfing fings."

"Iv that fo?" said Antioch, who had poked his head out of the shaggoir and spoken loud enough for everyone to hear.

The room went cold.

"Funny fing iv . . ." he went on, "I fink I've forgotten it. There'f another one I know . . . It'f about a man who goev into a fhop and the fign above the door readf 'Funeral director.'"

"What does 'suneral' mean?" asked an anonymous voice.

Ignoring the interruption, Willy went on: "Fo, he faid: Bonvour, can you direct me to fome fun? Ah!, faid he (alfo wiv a lifp), I can't do that, I only ftock bierv. Right, give me a pint!, he faid."

Willy piffed himfelf laughing.

Everyone had heard the joke before and greeted it with a smattering of embarrassed laughter.

"I fee you want more," Willy continued. "Here'v another one for you. But after that, it'll be fomeone elfe'v turn. What about you, Veorves?"

As Veorves took issue with this, Antioch groped behind his back and managed to get the record player plugged back in, and everyone resumed dancing as Willy, disheartened, shrugged and mumbled:

"It'f up to you, do av you will . . . I juft wanted to give the party a bit of atmofphere."

The Major grabbed his dancing partner again and Antioch went back to his shaggoir, where the recovering Zizanie was touching up her makeup.

CHAPTER X

In the middle of the forest of Marly, Fromental de Vercoquin, sitting beneath a rubber tree, had spent the last half hour swearing under his breath. He was swearing under his breath because he'd spent the half hour prior to that swearing out loud, and his left vocal cord had gotten stuck.

CHAPTER XI

On returning to the shaggoir, Antioch made out, atop the pile of jumbled coats in the corner of the room, four legs he'd not previously noticed. It was two individuals up there, checking their specific difference through the "fits" and "doesn't fit" calibration method, as recommended by the Office for Standardization in Mechanical Engineering.

The girl had beautiful knees, but also ginger hair, as Antioch observed when he looked up. He was shocked by the sight of that harsh color and prudishly looked away.

Antioch could see that the coat on top was a waterproof coat, so he left the intrepid physiology researchers in peace. To be fair, they weren't hurting anyone. At their age, it's good to conduct one's own research into questions of nature.

Antioch helped Zizanie adjust her dress, which looked ready to go off on its own, and they came back into the main room as if nothing had come of their absence. So little had come of it, in fact . . .

The Major was standing next to the record player, looking somber. Antioch went over to him.

"Go for it," he said.

"She's a proper lady, wouldn't you say?" said the Major.

"Certainly," said Antioch. "And even better than that, she's dexterous and has a delicate touch."

"I bet she's a virgin!" declared the Major.

"And twenty minutes ago," said Antioch, "you'd have won."

"I don't get it," said the Major. "But no matter. So, you think she's alright?"

"Perfectly alright, bud," said Antioch.

"Do you think I've got a chance?" added the Major, full of hope.

"Without a doubt, bud," his acolyte reassured him once more, before stopping to turn and watch a couple who were really swinging.

The male had a curly mop of hair and was wearing a sky-blue suit, the jacket of which went down to his shins. There were three vents in the back, seven gussets, two half-belts, one over the other, and just one button to fasten it up. The trousers, barely visible beneath the jacket, were so tight that the man's calves protruded obscenely from their strange sheaths. The collar of the jacket went up to the top of his ears. There was a small slit on each side, through which his ears could stick out. His tie was made from a single thread of rayon, knotted with no mean skill, and in his breast pocket was an orange and mauve handkerchief. His mustard-colored socks were the same color as the Major's, though worn with infinitely less elegance, and disappeared into his beige suede shoes, which looked as though they'd been victim to a thousand different bug bites. He was Swing.

The female was also wearing a jacket, which revealed at least a millimeter of the bottom of her ample pleated skirt of Mauritian gauze. She was superbly built, with restless buttocks atop short, fat legs, and she had sweaty armpits. Her outfit was less eccentric than her partner's and consequently attracted almost no attention: a bright red blouse, chocolate-colored silk tights, light-yellow pig-skin flats, with nine gold bracelets on her left wrist and a ring in her nose.

His name was Alexandre, but everyone called him Coco. Her name was Jacqueline. And her nickname was Coco.

Coco grabbed Coco by the left ankle and, after skillfully spinning her in the air, she landed with her legs straddling his left knee; then, sweeping his right leg over his partner's head, he suddenly let go of her, whereupon she found herself upright with her face turned toward his back. He instantly fell backward into a crab position and inserted his head between her thighs before quickly getting up, lifting her from the ground, and throwing her, headfirst, between his own legs, while finding himself in the same position, his back cushioned by his partner's breasts. He then flipped over to face her, shrieked "Yeah!," waved his index finger, took three steps back, four steps forward, eleven steps to the side, six steps in a circle, and two on his stomach, and started all over again. They were both sweating profusely, concentrating intensely, somewhat moved by the attention tinged with respect that was visible on the faces of the admiring spectators. They were very, very Swing.

Antioch sighed with regret. He was too old for this sort of stuff and his underpants were very ill-fitting.

He resumed his conversation with the Major.

"Why don't you invite her to dance?" he asked.

"I daren't ..." said the Major. "She intimidates me. She's too good for me."

Antioch went up to Zizanie, whose big eyes with dark shadows barely concealed the pleasure with which they watched him return.

"Hey," he said. "You've got to dance with the Major. He loves you."

"Oh! Don't tell me that now!" said Zizanie, visibly moved and worried.

"I promise you, it would be better if you did ... He's really nice, he's loaded, and he's a complete idiot: the perfect husband."

"What? I've got to marry him?"

"Why, of course," said Antioch, as though it were obvious.

CHAPTER XII

Fromental, who had decided to get up, was getting closer to the Major's house. He had only five miles and 1,400 yards to go. His left leg was hurting him. It may have been carrying a bit more than his right, as his tailor had always presumed that Fromental was normally endowed.

He got to Versailles just before 6:30 a.m. and saved ten minutes on his theoretical route on foot by taking a complicated series of blue and gray streetcars of an excessively noisy disposition.

The last of these dropped him not far from the foot of the hill known by cycling fans as the côte de Picardie.

He decided to try his hand at hitching a lift. On seeing a little old 3hp Zebraline approach with a portly lady at the wheel, he frantically waved his arms about.

She pulled up before him.

"Thank you, Madame," said Fromental. "Would you happen to be passing via Ville d'Avrille?"

"Why, no, Monsieur," said the lady. "Why on earth should I be going to Ville d'Avrille when I live here?"

"Of course, Madame," Fromental conceded.

He sloped off, with a heavy heart.

A hundred yards further on, he had climbed only a third of the way up the hill and his breathing was beginning to get labored. He stopped once more.

A car passed. It was a 1905 model Duguesclin, with pressure valves sticking out from the radiator and a wrecked rear axle.

It skidded to a halt less than a yard away (it was going uphill) and an old man with a bushy beard stuck his head out of the window.

"Absolutely, young man," he said, before Fromental could get his bearings. "Hop in. But before you do, could you give the crank handle a little turn?"

He had been turning the crank handle for twelve minutes when the car suddenly shot off the very moment he was going to open the car door to get in. The old man only managed to stop the thing at the top of the hill.

"Do forgive me," he said to Vercoquin, who had caught up with him in a jog. "She gets a bit feisty when we have warm weather."

"Only to be expected," said Fromental. "She's probably going through the change."

He got in and sat to the left of the old chap, and the Duguesclin sped down the hill at full tilt.

On reaching the bottom of the hill, the two left-side tires exploded.

"I really must get a new tailor," thought Fromental, for no good reason and with an incredible lack of logic.

The old man was furious.

"You're too heavy!" he shouted. "This is your fault. That's the first puncture I've had since 1911."

"On the same tires?" enquired Fromental, genuinely interested.

"Well, obviously! I've only had a car since last year. The tires are new!"

"So you were born in 1911?" asked Fromental, seeking to understand.

"Don't add insult to punctury!" the old man grumbled. "And get fixing those tires."

CHAPTER XIII

At that very instant, the Major, tenderly holding Zizanie's waist, was walking slowly down the house steps. He went down the right-hand path and came to the far end of the gardens at a leisurely pace, while feverishly trying to think of something to talk about.

The garden wall at this point was quite low, and eleven individuals wearing navy-blue suits and white socks were puking over the aforementioned wall, which conveniently served as an elbow rest.

"Well-mannered lads," remarked the Major as he walked past them. "They'd rather puke in my neighbor's garden. Though it's a shameful waste of good booze."

"My, you're mean!" said Zizanie, with a hint of reproach in her gentle voice.

"My dear!" said the Major. "For you, I should give all I have!"

"My, you're so generous," said Zizanie, with a smile and a hug.

The Major's heart swam in joy, with a great splashing sound like a porpoise. It was the sound of the outdoor vomitorium, but he was oblivious to that.

Their presence seemed to bother the eleven guys, whose backs seemed imbued with an air of reproach, so the Major and the beautiful blonde went quietly off down the garden path.

They sat down on the bench that Antioch had placed that morning in the shade of the pie-scraper. Zizanie was feeling a little sleepy. The Major slowly rested his head on his partner's shoulder, burying his nose in her golden hair, from which emanated an insidious perfume, a stale stench of rue Royale and place Vendôme. The perfume was Miss Vissera by Hernia.

The Major held his sweetheart's hands in his own, and his mind wandered off into a dream of stupefying bliss.

Something cold and moist on his right hand startled him and he cried out like a she-shnuff in ecstasy. Zizanie awoke.

On hearing the Major's squeal, the mackintosh, who had been licking the Major's hand, jumped twelve feet in the air, and then moved off, his feelings hurt, with a "Psssh!"

"Poor old thing!" said the Major. "I scared him."

"But he scared you, my dear," said Zizanie. "Your mackintosh is stupid."

"He's so young," sighed the Major. "And he loves me so much. But, Christ almighty! You just called me your 'dear!'"

"I did. Forgive me," said Zizanie. "You know, I was woken with a start."

"Don't apologize!" whispered the Major, full of ardor. "I belong to you."

"Let's sleep, my belonging!" decided Zizanie, getting back into a comfy position.

CHAPTER XIV

Antioch, left to his own devices, had just welcomed three latecomers, including, wonder of wonders, a splendid redhead with green eyes. The other two-thirds, a dude and dudette of no interest, had already headed straight for the bar. Antioch asked the redhead to dance.

"Do you know anyone here?" he said.

"No!" said the beautiful redhead. "And you?"

"Not everyone, unfortunately!" Antioch sighed, and he held her against his heart, emphatically.

"My name's Jacqueline!" she said, as she attempted to slide one of her thighs between Antioch's legs. He reacted accordingly and kissed her on the lips for the rest of the record: it was one of Crosse and Blackwell's latest hits, "Home Base after Midnight."

Antioch danced the next two numbers with his new partner and made sure not to let go of her during the short intervals that lasted from the end of one record to the beginning of the one that followed.

He was just getting ready for a third dance when some guy in a houndstooth suit came up to him, with a worried look on his face, and dragged him away upstairs.

"Look!" he said, pointing to the toilet door. "It's overflowing!" He tried to skedaddle.

"Not so fast . . ." said Antioch, holding him by the sleeve. "You come with me. It's no fun all alone."

Together, they went into the *buen retiro*. It was indeed overflowing. The rolled-up newspapers were clearly visible.

"So, if that's how it is . . ." said Antioch, rolling up his sleeves. "Let's unblock it, shall we? Roll up your sleeves!"

"But . . . you're already ready to . . ."

"Not at all! Mine are rolled up so I can smash your face in if the job's not finished by the time the little hand on the clock has gone round five times. You've got another thing coming," he added, "if you think you can teach an old preamble like me how to sail round Cape Horn . . ."

"Oh? . . ." said the guy as he plunged his fingers into something soft at the bottom of the U-bend, which made him shudder from head to toe and instantly turn a creamy shade of pale.

"There's a sink to your right," Antioch advised, at the precise moment when the wretch's head was beneath the window that his executioner had just opened. The window withstood the blow, as did the skull.

Antioch then went back downstairs.

Just as he had expected, Jacqueline was at the buffet, flanked by two individuals competing to pour her a drink. Antioch grabbed the glass that they had managed to fill and offered it to Jacqueline.

"Thanks!" she said with a smile and followed him to the middle of the dance floor, which, by some miracle, Corneille had just left.

He hugged her once more. Back at the buffet, the two individuals had quite a face on them.

"Well, would you look at that?" sniggered Antioch. "They've placenta behind their ears, and they want to get the better of a pro of my stature!"

"Is that so?" replied Jacqueline, not really knowing what he was talking about. "Oh, who's he?"

In the lounge doorway, Fromental had just appeared.

CHAPTER XV

Fortunately, "Mushrooms behind My Red Ears" had just started playing, and the unlucky Fromental's inflammatory roar was muffled by the din of the brass section. He ran to the bar and downed two-thirds of a bottle of gin before coming up for air.

Having instantly forgotten everything that happened, he gazed round at the partygoers, with the beatific grin of a goat that has just found hay in its hooves.

In one corner of the room, he spotted a dainty blonde, whose neckline plunged to the tips of her breasts, and he headed confidently toward her. Without waiting for him, she made it to the door. He followed her, running after her, occasionally bounding 6′8″ in the air to catch a little yellow butterfly. She disappeared—but not to everyone—into a clump of Hardian laurel, the branches of which closed over Fromental, who had dived in after her.

CHAPTER XVI

Having slept for half an hour, the Major, teased from his torpor by a distant roar—when Fromental entered the lounge—awoke with a start. Zizanie had also awoken.

He looked at her adoringly and noticed that her belly was swelling at an alarming rate.

"Zizanie!" he cried. "What's happening?"

"Oh, my love!" she said. "Is it possible for you to have behaved as you did while asleep and for you to not remember anything of it?"

"Fancy that!" said the Major insignificantly. "I didn't notice a thing. Forgive me, my love, but we're going to have to make this legit."

The Major was quite naïve when it came to matters of the heart and was unaware that it took at least ten days for it to show.

"It's quite simple," said Zizanie. "Today's Thursday. It's seven o'clock in the morning, Antioch can go see my uncle, who'll still be in his office, and ask for my hand in marriage on thy behalf."

"Prithee, why so formal, my Gregorian beauty?" asked the Major, who was moved to tears and shaking sporadically from his shoulder to his ischium.

"I'm sorry, darling," replied Zizanie. "Anyway, I've had a good think..."

"It's crazy what you can do while you're asleep," the Major cut in.

"I've had a good think about things and I reckon I'll never meet a better husband..."

"Oh, my angel, my life!" cried the Major. "You called me your darling... But why don't I go straight to your father to ask for your hand in marriage?"

"I have none."

"So he's family?"

"He's my mother's brother. He spends his life at his office."

"What does your aunt think about that?"

"He doesn't care. He doesn't even allow her to live with him. She lives in a small apartment where he goes to see her from time to time."

"Bloody bees-knees!" declared the Major.

"I'd prefer kiss-niece," murmured Zizanie, rubbing up against him. "After all, he is my uncle."

The joy with which the Major obeyed Zizanie was so barely concealed that it caused three buttons to pop, nearly blinding her in one eye.

"Let's go look for Antioch," she suggested, somewhat assuaged.

CHAPTER XVII

On walking past the laurel bush in which Fromental had just dived, the Major's head was struck successively by a sock, a left shoe, a pair of underpants, a pair of trousers—whereupon he realized who the flinger was—and then another sock, a right shoe, a pair of suspenders, a vest, and a shirt with the tie still round the collar. These items were followed immediately by a dress, a bra, a pair of women's shoes, a pair of stockings, a dainty lace belt ostensibly designed to keep said stockings in place, and a 69-carat ring fashioned from the sherd of some ancient menhir with gold edging and mounted on needle bearings. The ring almost blinded the mackintosh in one eye, as he had happened along at that instant, and he left with a "Psssh!"

From the avalanche described above, the Major deduced:

1. That they had used Fromental's jacket to lie on.

2. That his partner had not been wearing any knickers and therefore had known that it was going to be a nice surprise party.

He might have deduced a whole load of other things but stopped there.

He was pleased that people were enjoying themselves at his party.

He was also happy to see that Fromental had had his mind taken off his car.

CHAPTER XVIII

It should be added that Fromental had not yet seen his car.

CHAPTER XIX

Using the property of Zizanie's dress, which had first drawn Antioch's attention to her, the Major traced a direct line back to the house. The result this yielded was excellent.

He climbed the steps and shouted: "Antioch!"

Said individual did not answer and the Major lost no time in understanding that he was not there. Consequently, the Major entered the house and headed straight for the shaggoir. He left Zizanie on the doorstep.

He soon found Antioch, who stood up, satisfied, as it was his eleventh helping of "seconds," and it still did not seem to be enough. Jacqueline conscientiously pulled down the hem of her skirt and got up, full of enthusiasm.

"D'you want to dance?" she suggested to the Major, with her eyes tilted at an angle of 1,300 degrees.

"Just a minute . . ." begged the Major.

"It's okay, I'll try and find someone else . . ." she said as she drifted off, full of discretion and goat hair from the sofa in the shaggoir.

"Antioch!" moaned the Major as soon as she had scarper-flown away.

"Present!" answered Antioch, standing stiffly and impeccably to attention, his torso at a right angle, and index finger to his carotid.

"I've got to marry her, right now . . . She's . . ."

"What!?" exclaimed Antioch. "Already!?"

"Yes . . ." the Major sighed, modestly. "And I didn't even realize. It all happened when I was asleep."

"You're an amazing guy!" said Antioch.

"Thanks, old man," said the Major. "Can I count on you?"

"To ask her father for her hand in marriage, you mean?"

"No, her uncle."

"And where does that vertebrate hang out?" asked Antioch.

"In his office, surrounded by his collection of precious documents covering all activities of human industry of no interest whatsoever."

"Very well!" said Antioch. "I'll go tomorrow."

"You'll go now!" insisted the Major. "Look at her belly."

"And?" said Antioch, having half-opened the shaggoir door to give her a look. "What's so special?"

Indeed, Zizanie's belly was quite flat, as the Major, in turn, had chance to observe.

"What the hell!" he said. "She's pulled the old pylorus trick on me . . ."

It was a trick performed by fakirs, requiring years of training, and involved causing the stomach to swell to almost inhuman proportions.

"Perhaps you were just seeing things," said Antioch. "Understandable after an encounter like that . . ."

"You must be right," conceded the Major. "My nerves are corkscrewing. You can go and find her uncle tomorrow."

CHAPTER XX

In the lounge, where the dancers were still evolving, the Major found Zizanie again, but Antioch did not manage to find Jacqueline. So he went out to the gardens and noticed a foot sticking out from behind a tree . . . attached to this foot, he found a party guest, quite pale and clearly exhausted . . . further on, he found another guest in the same state, and then five more, all muddled together, and two more on their own.

He finally saw the redhead in the vegetable garden with her hands on a leek and trying out the Macedonian strong-arm technique.

He called out to her. She let her skirt fall back into place and, full of energy, headed over to him.

"Still Swing?" he asked her.

"Why, naturally . . . What about you?"

"Still got it, but not much left . . ."

"My poor love," she whispered affectionately, reaching up to give him a hug.

There was the sinister sound of something snapping and Antioch stuck his right hand successively into both of his trouser legs, and pulled out the two halves of a heinously shredded pair of underpants.

"I'm not the man for the . . . job" he confessed. "But given that, I may know someone who'll be to your satisfaction . . ."

Escorting her by the arm at a respectful distance, they arrived at the laurel bush in the middle of which Fromental, completely naked, seemed to be fornicating with the soil. His endeavors had been so spirited that his conquest, by dint of the repeated pressure, had gradually disappeared beneath a thick layer of humus, and was sinking further and further into the loam.

Having extricated her from that uncomfortable position, Antioch left her to come round on the fresh grass, and then orchestrated the introductions.

CHAPTER XXI

On his 114th attempt, Fromental collapsed, vanquished, onto Jacqueline's fragrant body as she sniffed dubiously at a sprig of laurel.

CHAPTER XXII

The surprise party was drawing to a close. Janine had managed to hide the twenty-nine records that she had carefully handpicked over the course of the afternoon in her bra. Corneille, long gone to eat some homemade stew, had come back, then gone again, and nobody knew where he was. His stricken parents were going round in circles in the middle of the room, and everyone thought they were doing some new swing dance.

Antioch headed to the floors upstairs. He removed two couples from the Major's bed, two others and a pederast from his own bed, three from the broom cupboard, and one from the shoe cupboard (they were a very small couple). He found seven girls and one guy in the coal cellar, all naked and covered in mauve vomitus. He pulled a small brunette from the boiler tank, which luckily had not yet quite cooled down, and so had saved her from catching pneumonia; gathered 10 francs and 45 centimes in cash from shaking a chandelier in which two inebriated individuals of indeterminable gender had been playing bridge, unnoticed, since 5:00; swept up the pieces from 762 cut-crystal glasses that had been smashed since the party began. He found bits of cake everywhere, even on plates, a makeup compact in the toilet-paper dispenser, a pair of unmatching checked woolen shoes from the electric oven, freed a hunting dog—which he had never seen before—from the pantry, and extinguished six nascent fires caused by the persistent dropping of cigarette butts. Three of the four sofas in the dance room were stained with port; the fourth with mayonnaise. The record player had lost its arm as well as its motor. All that was left of it was the power switch.

Antioch got back to the main room just as the guests were leaving. There were three raincoats left over.

He said goodbye to everyone and went to wait for them at the gate, where he got some revenge by shooting one in four of them down with a Tommy gun as they left the premises. After that, he climbed the path back to the house and walked past the laurel bush.

The mackintosh, astride a passed-out Jacqueline, was whimpering with joy. Antioch stroked him with the palm of his hand, dressed Fromental, who was still not moving, as well as his initial partner, who was asleep on the lawn, and woke them by giving them both a good kick up the backside.

"Where's my car?" asked Fromental, recovering consciousness.

"There," said Antioch, pointing to a pile of debris crowned by a crooked steering wheel.

Fromental sat himself behind the wheel and got the young girl to sit beside him.

"Debriekas always fire up with a simple turn of the key," he bellowed.

He pulled a lever and the steering wheel raced off, with Fromental hanging on . . .

The little blonde went running after him . . .

END OF PART I

PART II

In the Shadow of the Roneos

CHAPTER I

Chief Junior Engineer Léon-Charles Miqueut was chairing his weekly meeting with his six deputies in his stinking office on the top floor of a modern, freestone building.

The room was furnished, in exquisite taste, with sixteen filing cabinets made from sodomized oak and coated with bureaucratic varnish reminiscent of goose poop, steel cabinets with drawers on rollers filled with particularly confidential papers, tables overflowing with urgent documents and a weekly planning schedule, three meters by two in size, featuring a finely tuned system of multicolored cards that were never updated. Ten or so shelves held the fruits of that department's laborious activity—made concrete in the form of little mouse-grey folders—which aimed to regulate every sphere of human activity. They were called "Nothons." Their arrogant aim was to organize production and to protect consumers.

In the hierarchy, Chief Junior Engineer Miqueut was one grade immediately below Chief Engineer Touchebœuf. They both dealt with technical matters.

The job of looking after administrative issues fell, naturally, to the Chief of Administration, Joseph Brignole, together, in part, with the General Secretary.

The General Chairman and Managing Director, Émile Gallopin, was responsible for coordinating his subordinates' tasks. Another ten or so admin staff of various stripes made up the unit, which was named the NATIONAL CONSORTIUM FOR STANDARDIZATION or, for short, the N.C.S.

The building was also home to a number of other General Inspectors, an old gang of pensioners who spent the vast majority of their time snoring through technical meetings, and the rest of their time roaming the land on the pretext of carrying out missions, which enabled them to extort enough subscriptions from members to just about keep the N.C.S. going.

To stop the N.C.S. from going over the top, the Government—unable to put the brakes on Chief Engineers Miqueut and Touchebœuf's zeal for developing Nothons—had appointed a brilliant graduate of the illustrious École Polytechnique to represent it and to oversee the Consortium. Known as Central Government Delegate Requin, it was his job to delay the development of Nothons as much as he possibly could. He achieved this with ease by summoning N.C.S. heads to his office several times every week for constantly rehashed discussions; thanks to this routine, the constant rehashing had become a near necessity.

Apart from that, Requin siphoned money from an assortment of Ministries and put his own name to technical works produced by little-known members of staff who spent many a painful hour writing them.

Yet despite the Government, despite the obstacles, despite everything, the fact remained that at the end of each month a few more Nothons had been passed. Without the prudent precautions taken by manufacturers and retailers, the situation would have proven dangerous. What would other countries think of a place where 100 centiliters were provided for a liter, or where an anchor bolt guaranteed to resist 15 tons did not shear under a load of 15,000 kilos? Fortunately, the relevant professions, with Government support, played a significant part in creating Nothons, and they were designed in such a way that it took years to decrypt them. As soon as that happened, they entered a process of revision.

To keep the Government Delegate happy, Miqueut and Touchebœuf had also made some effort to curb the enthusiasm of their underlings and to stem any progress in the development of Nothons. However, recognizing that they were completely harmless, the two Chief Engineers confined themselves to making frequent recommendations by way of precaution. As a way of maximizing the amount of time wasted, they followed Government Delegate Requin's lead and organized more and more meetings.

Thanks to an effective propaganda campaign, moreover, Nothons were extremely unpopular with the general public—whom they were supposed to protect.

CHAPTER II

"Right then!" muttered Miqueut, not very well endowed when it came to the gift of the gab . . . "Erm . . . Today, er, I'm going to talk to you about . . . er . . . a number of things, to which I think it will be useful to draw . . . well, at least some of those things, your attention, once more."

He scrutinized each of his colleagues with the eyes of a mole that had been partying all night long, wet his lips with whitish saliva, and continued:

"To begin with, the question of commas . . . I have noticed, and not infrequently . . . and please note that I am not talking specifically about our department, where, *au contraire*, with the odd exception, admittedly, they are generally used with care, that the absence of commas can, in some instances, prove particularly troublesome ... As you know, commas, which are used, within the sentence that one is writing, to mark a rest that must be observed, insofar as is possible, by the voice of the person reading, in such case, obviously, where the document is to be read out loud ... So, in short, I should like to remind you that great care is needed with commas because, and above all, in such case, as it were, where documents due to be sent to the Delegation are involved."

The Delegation was the Government body headed by Requin, responsible for assessing the proposals and projects for Nothons that emerged from the N.C.S. It scared Miqueut half to death, as it represented the Government's Administration.

Miqueut stopped talking. He always turned somewhat pale and solemn-looking when he talked about the Delegation, and consequently lowered the pitch of his voice significantly.

"Let me remind you, particularly with regard to reports, that it is necessary, therefore, to be very careful, and I expect all of you to do what it takes to not lose sight of this reflection that, I repeat, does not apply to our department, where, in general, with just a few exceptions, we're quite careful. I was talking, recently, with someone who considers these problems frequently, and I can assure you that what counts when it comes to Nothons is the text that accompanies them and presents them, and, of course, there's ... er ... every interest in being as careful as possible, because, in our relations with others, and particularly, I'd like to underline this point, with the Delegation, we must resist the temptation to make jokes, because that would be liable to cause problems, and if that happens, well, that's another matter ... and, anyhow, I strongly urge you not to rely on our inspection unit, whose job it is to inspect, but which should, in fact, have nothing to do, and, indeed, some of you, with whom I've discussed this, have realized too late that it is somewhat risky to rely on the inspection unit, which, I repeat, is there to inspect, but, in fact, should have nothing left to inspect when they receive the documents."

He stopped talking, quite content, and looked around the table at the six deputies who were all nodding off and listening to him serenely, with the hint of a smile on their lips.

"In short . . ." he went on. "I repeat, it is necessary to be very careful. And now, I should like to talk to you about another matter that is almost as important as the issue of commas, and that is the issue of semicolons . . ."

Three hours later, the weekly meeting which, as a rule, was supposed to last ten minutes, was still underway and Miqueut was saying:

"Well, I think that . . . er . . . we've just about gone over everything in this morning's schedule . . . Would any of you like to raise any other issue that we might consider?"

"Yes, Monsieur," said Adolphe Troude, who awoke with a start. "There's the matter of the office copies of the weekly comics."

"What's up?" asked Miqueut.

"People are hogging them," said Troude. "The typists snaffle them from us, and the General Inspectors keep them for ages."

"You know that we must all show the greatest deference, as much me as you, toward the General Inspectors, who are old stalwarts of the first order . . ."

"That's no reason," said Troude, with no apparent logic, "for the typists to snaffle *Le Petit Illustré* from us."

"At any rate, you've done the right thing in raising this with me," said Miqueut, who made a note of the information in his special notepad. "I shall bring this matter up with Madame Lougre . . . Is there anything else?"

"No," said Troude, and the others shook their heads.

"As such, gentlemen, this meeting is adjourned . . . Léger, could I have a quick word with you?"

"Right away," said Léger. "I'll just go and get my notepad."

CHAPTER III

Having rushed back to his office, Léger briefly fingered his little moustache, which had been nibbled by moths over the winter, owing to a shortage of paradichlorobenzene caused by a flu epidemic which had just spread through the region of Lyon. He adjusted his salmon-colored gaiters, grabbed a thick pile of mail marked "urgent," smacked it against his thighs to get rid of the layer of dust on it, and ran out to Miqueut's office.

"Here we are, Monsieur," he said, as he sat to the left of this formidable man. "I've prepared the 127 replies for the morning's mail and I've compiled 32 memos for the Delegation that you asked me to have ready for tomorrow."

"Perfect!" said Miqueut. "And did you manage to type up the 654-page duplicated copy that we received the day before yesterday?"

"Mademoiselle Rouget is still working on it," said Léger. "I've given her a bit of a prod . . . I'm not too happy with her work."

"Indeed," said Miqueut. "It's dragging a little. When times are better, we'll try to get you a secretary up to the job. For the time being, however, we'll have to make do with what we have. So, let's see these letters."

"The first," said Léger, "is the reply to the Institute of Rubber regarding the trials for ice packs."

Chief Junior Engineer Miqueut adjusted his spectacles and read:

"'Dear Sir,

"'In reply to your letter, reference above, I . . .'

"No," he said. "Put 'We have the honor to acknowledge receipt of your letter, reference above' . . . That's the standard phrasing, you see . . ."

"Of course!" said Léger. "Forgive me. I forgot."

Miqueut carried on reading:

"'. . . we have the honor of informing you that . . .'

"That's fine," he approved. "You've grasped the phrasing. And actually, your first draft might suffice . . . Leave it as it was, eh . . .

"'. . . of informing you that we are planning, quite soon, to proceed with trials for ice packs under normal conditions of use. We should be grateful to you if you would let us know . . .'

"No, well, in short, they're the ones who depend, to a greater or lesser extent, on us, not the other way round, and we shouldn't be too . . . er . . . toadyish, say . . . well, no, that's not quite the word . . . but you understand what I'm driving at, don't you?"

"Yes . . ." replied Léger.

"Put something else, will you? I'm counting on you . . . Put 'Would you please' . . . or . . . well, you know . . .

"'. . . please let us know . . .'

"You sort it out, will you . . ."

"'. . . if you will be able to attend this meeting, which will also be attended by His Eminence Cardinal Baudrillon and the Head of Latex and Communications for the Central Ministry of Peat Bogs and Waterways, as well as the Inspector of Innocent Games for the Department of the Seine. Please let us know . . .'

"That's another 'please let us know' if the preceding sentence is changed," noted Léger with his eagle eye.

"Well . . . erm . . . You'll sort it out, won't you? I trust you to . . . er . . .

"'. . . inform us as soon as possible if you will be able to attend . . .'

"Oh, really! No, no," Miqueut exclaimed. "Your draft is no good . . ."

He armed himself with the grubby stub end of a management pencil—a brand supplied exclusively to the Consortium's executives—and in his cramped handwriting began writing between the lines:

"'. . .to inform us, as a matter of urgency'—You see . . .—'if it will be possible for you to attend . . .'

"Do you understand? Like that, in short, it's more . . . well, you get the idea . . ."

"Yes, Monsieur," replied Léger.

"So," Miqueut concluded with a quick scan of the rest of the letter, "your letter's perfectly fine apart from that . . . Let's have a look at the others . . ."

He was cut short by the ringing of his internal telephone.

"Oh, drat!" he said, raising his arms as a sign of his frustration.

He answered the phone.

"Hello? Yes! Hello there, my dear fellow! . . . What, now? Fine! I'll come down right away!

"They need me for a card game," he said with an apologetic shrug. "I'll look through the others with you, later . . ."

"Very well, Monsieur," replied Léger, who left the office and closed the door behind him.

CHAPTER IV

The departments under Chief Junior Engineer Miqueut were all on the top floor of the building that housed the whole Consortium. A number of connecting offices, which could be accessed by communicating doors, were served by a central corridor. At the very barycenter was the office of Léon-Charles, in pride of place, who was flanked by René Vidal to the right and Emmanuel Pigeon to the left. Next to Vidal's office was that of Victor Léger, which he shared with Henri Levadoux. Pigeon was opposite Adolphe Troude, and next to them was Jacques Marion, whose office was at one end of the corridor. Opposite were the offices for the typists and switchboard operators.

Léger made his exit via Vidal's office.

"He's gone downstairs!" he announced on his way through.

Vidal had already heard Miqueut leave his office, stop to urinate in the toilet, which he did without fail every time he went out, and head for the stairs. Pigeon, whose hearing was excellent, joined the two others, and Levadoux's arrival completed the assembly.

Whenever Chief Junior Engineer Miqueut went downstairs to talk with Touchebœuf or attend a meeting, it was in Vidal's office that they congregated.

Ordinarily, Adolphe Troude would stay in his office and cover sheet after sheet of old plans for canceled Nothons with doodles that looked like the nocturnal meditations of an illiterate, dipsomaniacal hymenopteran.

Marion was asleep, his chin resting comfortably on the end of a ruler made from the wood of a pear tree with a cleft in it. He had just remarried, and it seemed as though things were not going as well as he had hoped. Before joining the N.C.S., he had, it is true, spent a long time in the army, and the confusion between the martial and the marital was perhaps having an impact.

"Gentlemen," declared Pigeon. "Our previous meetings have yielded valuable information regarding the habits of Chief Junior Engineer Miqueut. To summarize what we have found, here is what we now know thanks to our own observations:

a) He says, "Looking forward to seeing you again," on the phone;
b) He frequently uses the well-known expression, "in such a way that";
c) He scratches the area around his trouser fly;
d) He only stops scratching to bite his fingernails.

"Agreed," replied Vidal.

"However," Pigeon went on, "recent reflection on my part obliges me to affirm that we are not in agreement on this last point . . . He does *not* bite his fingernails."

"He's always sucking on his fingers!" Léger protested.

"That's correct," Pigeon replied firmly. "But only after he's put them up his nose. Such is his *modus operandi*: with a view to sharpening his nails, he rubs them against his teeth, and then he puts them up his nose, wherefrom he pulls them out with their load. Using the snot covering the ends of his phalanges, he smooths his moustache, and then savors the fruits of his research."

"Motion carried!" said Levadoux.

"No further comment."

"Nothing for now."

"But even so!" concluded Vidal. "It's all so boring!"

"It's crazy how boring it all is!" agreed Pigeon.

"It would be so lovely to be out in the fresh air!" said Levadoux. The originality of this comment fogged the depths of his burnt topaz-colored eyes with a cloud of galloping nostalgia.

"I for one am not bored," said Léger. "In fact, I've just realized, thanks to the canniest of calculations that I found in the *French Bulletin of Heretical Insurance Consultants*, that I've already lived more than half of my expected existence. The worst is over."

On this consolatory conclusion, they parted company. Pigeon went back to his office to have a nap, Victor went back to his English lessons, and Levadoux resumed his studies for the tough See-Pee-Hey exam he was due to sit at the end of the year. Indeed, his plan was to leave the N.C.S., and the fact of having the See-Pee-Hey qualification would come in very handy and make things easier when he wanted to return, sometime later.

René Vidal went back to copying out a few musical scores. He played *trompette harmonique* in Claude Abadie's amateur jazz band, which was very time-consuming.

Only incidentally did they spend their time drafting Nothon projects for which Chief Junior Engineer Miqueut, whose generous heart knew no equal, took complete credit as soon as they were ready.

CHAPTER V

Back in his office, alone, René Vidal resumed the task that had been occupying him. It involved perforating a certain number of slips of paper used for assessment purposes.

He had been making holes in the assessment slips for barely ten minutes when the internal telephone began to gurgle.

He answered it.

"Hello? Monsieur Vidal? It's Mademoiselle Alliage."

"Hello, Mademoiselle," said Vidal.

"Hello, Monsieur. We have a visitor here, Monsieur, who wishes to see Monsieur Miqueut."

"Regarding what, exactly?" asked Vidal.

"Something to do with white gloves, but it's not easy to understand what he's saying."

"White gloves?" mumbled Vidal. "Leather or fabric . . . ? Fine, I'll deal with him. Send him up, please, Mademoiselle. I'll see him, as Monsieur Miqueut is in a meeting. What's the fellow's name?"

"It's Monsieur Tambrétambre, Monsieur. Right then, I'll send him up to you."

"Very well."

Vidal hung up.

"What a pain, guys," he said, sticking his head round the door to the office of Léger and Levadoux. "I've got a visitor."

"Ha! Have a good time!" jibed Léger who, with no segue whatsoever, started proclaiming, "My tailor is rich!" It was the first sentence he had learned in his English course.

With a circular, centripetal movement of his right arm, Vidal swept up the mess on top of his desk and stuffed the resulting pile of paperwork into the left-hand drawer, which made the office look more distinguished. He then picked up a duplicate copy of some document and began to read it studiously. He always used the same one for this purpose. He had had it for seven years, but it was very thick and looked very serious. It dealt with the standardization of pins for the rear wheels of light-transport vans used to deliver building materials smaller than 17 × 30 × 15 centimeters that posed no significant danger in their handling. The matter remained unresolved, but the document was unusable.

There were two knocks at his door.

"Enter!" Vidal shouted.

Antioch entered.

"Hello, Monsieur," said Vidal. "Please, take a seat."

He pushed a chair toward him.

The two men looked at each other for a moment and noticed that they looked strangely alike, which put them both very much at ease.

"Monsieur," said Antioch. "I should like to see Monsieur Miqueut regarding a personal matter. In fact, I'd like to ask him for the hand of his niece in marriage."

"Please allow me to congratulate you . . ." said René Vidal, trying to hide a pitying smile.

"No need for that. I'm asking on behalf of a friend," Antioch added quickly.

"Well, well! If this is the sort of favor you do for friends, I should be forever grateful if you could see me, henceforth, as a potential enemy," said Vidal in the style so characteristic of the N.C.S.

"In other words," deduced Antioch, who preferred less sophisticated language, "our Junior Engineer Miqueut is a bit of a shit bag."

"The worst there is," said Vidal.

At that moment, the communicating door to the office of Levadoux and Léger opened suddenly.

"Sorry to interrupt," said Levadoux, sticking his head through the gap between the door and its frame. "You wouldn't know what Miqueut's up to later, would you?"

"I think he's off to a meeting with Troude," said Vidal. "But if I were you, I'd check first."

"Thanks!" said Levadoux, shutting the door behind him.

"Right. Back to business," said Antioch. "I guess I've had a stroke of luck in not getting to meet Miqueut this morning? It's always better to find out about the people you're dealing with before you meet them."

"You're right, there," said Vidal. "But I have to say I wasn't even aware Miqueut had a niece."

"She's alright, really ..." Antioch admitted, thinking back to the party.

"Well, in that case, she has nothing in common with her uncle."

They were, indeed, different. Miqueut's features resembled a cross between a grizzly gherkin and a Chinese person, not least because of the most unpleasant way in which he blinked his eyes; he was, in fact, short-sighted and, out of vanity, would often be seen without his glasses.

"You're starting to scare me," said Antioch. "Even so, the Major can handle it."

"Aha! So, you're acting on behalf of the Major?" said Vidal.

"D'you know him?"

"As if I were his father. And everyone knows the Major. Well, then ... I'd rather not carry on talking with you about my beloved boss any longer because I hate speaking ill of people. Would you like me to book a meeting for you, for later? Say, 3:00 p.m.? He'll still be here."

"Deal!" said Antioch. "I'm staying in this part of town. But I'll pop up to see you before I go in to see him. See you later, pal. And thanks!"

"See you later!" said Vidal, standing up once more in order to shake hands.

Antioch left the office and bumped into a lad aged five or six who was charging down the corridor like an onager in the wilds of Canada.

The boy had been recruited by Levadoux as a spy to keep an eye on Miqueut, night and day, to enable him to know when he could bunk off and go for a drink or seek out women of ill-repute. During the daytime, Levadoux would hide the boy in his office.

René Vidal, having sat down again at his desk, recovered the pile of paperwork that he had stuffed into the left-hand drawer and restored it to the sunlight.

Five minutes later, he heard what sounded like the scurrying of a rabbit in the corridor, and then the door to Miqueut's office slammed shut. He was back.

CHAPTER VI

Vidal half-opened the communicating door and said to his boss, "I saw someone, earlier, Monsieur, who had come here to see you."

"About what?" asked the Chief Junior Engineer.

"A certain Monsieur . . . Tambrétambre, I believe his name was, wished to make an appointment to see you. I suggested he come back later, at 3:00 p.m. You'd told me that you'd be free then."

"Quite . . ." said Miqueut. "You were right, but . . . er, as a rule, right, may I remind you that you should always ask me first before booking appointments for me. You know my diary's quite full and it might have been that I wasn't perhaps free after all; you see, as far as people outside are concerned, that would look very bad. We have to be very careful. Even so, this time, you hear, I approve of your actions, but in future, in short, be very careful."

"Very well, Monsieur," said Vidal.

"Have you nothing else to show me?"

"I've redrafted Cassegraine's report on pigs' ears as a Nothon."

"Perfect. I'd like you to show me that. Not right now, as I have an appointment . . . what about tomorrow, for example?"

He opened up his wallet and pulled out a special index card on which he wrote the day, the time, and the place of all his appointments.

"Let's see . . . Tomorrow . . ." he mumbled. "No, tomorrow morning, Léger and I are going to the Office of Perished Rubber, and tomorrow afternoon . . . But, in fact, this afternoon, even, I can't see this Tambrétambre fellow . . . You see, Vidal, I told you not to arrange appointments without consulting me first. This afternoon, I've got to go to the HQ of the Chewing-Gummers to hear a talk by Professor Dullard. I can't see this fellow . . . There's a lot of movement in the rubber industry, at the moment."

"I'll phone him, then," said Vidal, who had no intention whatsoever of phoning him.

"Good, but, you see, it would have been better, in short, if you'd consulted me first. The thing is, it would have avoided us wasting time, which is always a threat to the efficient running of the department . . ."

"What date should I give him for the appointment?" Vidal enquired.

Miqueut consulted his index cards. A good fifteen minutes elapsed.

"Right!" he said. "The 19th of March, between 3:07 and 3:13 pm ... And tell him to be punctual."

It was the 11th of February ...

CHAPTER VII

René Vidal rushed off to not make a phone call. He didn't know Antioch's phone number and all he had wanted to do was to avoid a tedious sermon from Miqueut on the importance of asking people one has contact with for the information required to get in touch with them, which may, in some cases, prove useful.

It was not long before Miqueut opened the door again.

"My telephone looks wrecked," he said. "It's annoying me. Would you get Levadoux for me?"

"He's just left his office, Monsieur," replied Vidal (who knew full well that Levadoux had done a runner an hour since). "I heard him go out."

"As soon as he gets back, tell him what's up, and ask him to come and see me."

"Absolutely, Monsieur," said Vidal.

CHAPTER VIII

While all this was going on, the Major, wearing a houndstooth-brush suit and the flattest cap he possessed, was walking up and down his garden paths, looking melancholic. He was waiting for Antioch, the bearer of good news, to return.

The mackintosh was following three meters behind him, looking even more melancholic, and chewing a cigarette paper he had found.

The Major suddenly pricked an ear. He recognized the distinctive tune of the Kanibal-Super that Antioch—who went everywhere by motorbike—was riding: three long notes were followed by three breves and then a fermata in G major.

Antioch raced up the path and joined the Major.

"Victory!" he cried. "I've . . ."

"You've seen Miqueut?" the Major interjected.

"No . . . But I'm going to see him this afternoon."

"Ah!" sighed the Major, bitterly. "But what if . . .?"

"You should be ashamed," said Antioch. "What a baboo you are!"

"Don't be cruel," begged the Major. "When are you seeing him?"

"At three!" replied Antioch.

"Can I come with you?"

"I didn't ask . . ."

"Make a call, I beg you. I want to come."

"Yesterday, you didn't."

"What does that matter? That was yesterday . . ." said the Major with a heavy sigh.

"Alright, I'll phone . . ." Antioch consented.

He came back fifteen minutes later.

"It's fine for you to come along!" he said.

"I'll go and get changed!" cried the Major, jumping in the fullness of his joy.

"There's no rush . . . The appointment's booked for the 19th of March . . ."

"Shit!" concluded the Major. "What a pain in the ass."

He would always feel bad afterward for making such coarse remarks.

"So," he said, sighing in a way that was quite moving, "I'll not see Zizanie for more than a month . . ."

"Why's that?" asked Antioch.

"I promised I'd not see her again until I'd asked her uncle for her hand . . ." the Major explained.

"That was a stupid promise!" Antioch observed.

The mackintosh, seemingly of the same opinion, shook his head disparagingly and emitted a "Psssh!" full of scorn.

"What's bugging my balls," the Major added, "is not knowing what that awful, unrelenting low-life Fromental is up to."

"What's that got to do with anything, given that it's you she loves?" asked Antioch.

"I'm worried and perturbed . . ." said the Major. "I'm afraid . . ."

"You're losing your touch!" said Antioch, thinking back to the obvious insouciance that his friend had exhibited in the perilous episode of the quest for the forked barbarin.

And time passed . . .

CHAPTER IX

On the 16th of March, Miqueut called Vidal into his office.

"Vidal," he said. "It was you, I believe, who met this Monsieur . . . Tambrétambre, wasn't it? I trust that you made a note, as I have always advised you to do, of the reason for his visit. So please write it up for me . . . summarizing the main points to remember and, next to each one, the appropriate response . . . you see . . . so, in short . . . something concise, but sufficiently explicit . . ."

"Certainly, Monsieur," said Vidal.

"You can see why it's important," Miqueut went on, "to make a note, on a day-to-day basis, of one's telephone conversations and to keep written records of any meetings one might have, with a summary of the main points discussed. It just shows you the benefits that can accrue from it."

"Yes, Monsieur," said Vidal.

"And so, you see, it's extremely useful, after a meeting such as that, to record and retain any interesting ideas you might glean from a conversation, and to make up a little personal file, which you can copy and pass on to me, of course, in such a way that I might be aware of everything that's happening in the department when I happen not to be here, and, in short, er . . . it's very useful.

"But, apart from that . . ." Miqueut continued, "how are you getting on with your work?"

"I've drafted fifteen or so Nothon projects that I can give you, as soon as you have a spare minute . . ." said Vidal. "There are a few letters—not very urgent—to look at, as well."

"Ah, yes! Alright, if you like, we can talk more about this, later on."

"Call me when you're ready, Monsieur," Vidal suggested.

"That's the stuff, my good Vidal. Here, take these newspapers and pass them round the staff . . . and then send Levadoux up to see me."

At that precise moment, forewarned by his spy of Miqueut's return to the department, Levadoux was running up the stairs, and he reached his desk the very second Vidal was opening his office door.

Miqueut welcomed Levadoux warmly, but no sooner had he entered than Miqueut was called away to attend to some urgent matter on the fourth floor: Chief Engineer Touchebœuf needed a fourth player to make up a hand (for a bridge-based game) which was played every morning in the Director General's office, with a view to deciding who should deal with a certain series of Nothon projects that nobody would claim as their responsibility.

Levadoux went back to his office, livid. On his way there, he bumped into Vidal.

"What's wrong, pal?" he asked him.

"He's bugging me," replied Levadoux. "For once, I was here, and he buzzes off just when we were going to start doing something."

"He really is a bugger!" agreed Emmanuel who, having heard Miqueut leave his office, just happened to come along.

"He's bugging all of us," Victor chimed in, energetically, his pure lips being unable, despite such energy, to issue any ruder word than that. "But, to be fair, it's not too bad being bugged by someone else. It's a lot less tiring than getting bugged by yourself."

"Filthy capitalist!" said Vidal. "Come the revolution . . ."

René Vidal and Victor Léger had been students together and often made the most of that fact to exchange friendly words with each other.

They went their separate ways, because some secretaries were going into Miqueut's office to do some filing and, just to be careful, it was better to avoid any gossip.

Levadoux looked at his notepad, deduced that, in all probability, Miqueut would be gone for at least an hour, and bunked off.

Five minutes later, his boss, having rushed back owing to some unforeseen interruption of the card game, opened Vidal's office door.

"Is Levadoux not around?" he asked, with a uterine smile.

"He's just left his office, Monsieur. I believe he may've gone over to rue du Trente-neuf-Juillet."

There was an annex of the N.C.S. there.

"How annoying!" said Miqueut.

In absolute terms, it was all the more annoying because completely false.

"Send him to see me as soon as he gets back," barked Miqueut.

"Certainly, Monsieur," said Vidal.

CHAPTER X

It just so happened that the 19th of March fell on a Monday.

At a quarter to nine, Miqueut gathered his six deputies around him for the weekly meeting.

When they were all seated, forming an attentive semicircle before him, each one holding a pen or a pencil in their right hand, and with a blank sheet of paper on their left knee destined to record in writing the fruits of Miqueut's prolific intellectual labors, the Chair cleared the depths of his throat, the better to speak more clearly, and began in these terms:

"Right! Erm ... Today, I'm going to talk to you about something important ... that is to say, the matter of telephones. As you know, we have only a few lines at our disposal ... now, of course, when the N.C.S. has grown, when we are sufficiently known and when our premises match our stature, with a base, for example, in a district of Paris, which is planned, moreover, when our finances are better ... which, I hope, will one day be the case ... er ... given that, however ... in light, in short, of the importance of what we do ... right, in short, I advise you to only use the telephone with the utmost discretion, and I refer, in particular, to personal calls ... Please note, by the way, that my point is general in nature ... In our department, we don't take the biscuit, but I have been informed of the case of one staff member, from another department, who has received two personal calls in one year ... well, in short, that takes the biscuit. And you should only make a call if it's absolutely necessary, and keep it as short as possible. As you can understand, when outside agencies call us, I mean official bodies in particular, as well as those, in general, whose good favor we should aspire to win, and when, in short, no line is available ... Well! It makes a bad impression ... Particularly if the caller is Requin himself. And so, I wanted to draw your attention to what ... to ... well ... there is much to be gained from minimizing one's use of the telephone, except, of course, in cases of emergency or when using the telephone is absolutely necessary ... Furthermore, you are aware that while a telephone call is cheaper than a standard letter, a call becomes more expensive when it goes on for longer than a certain time, and that, ultimately, a call ends up being deducted from the N.C.S. budget."

"What we could do," suggested Troude, "is reduce the pressure on the lines by using pneumatic letters ..."

"Don't even think about it," countered Miqueut. "A pneumatic letter costs three francs a pop; so, as you see, that would be impossible. No, in short, what we need to do, by way of reminder, is to be very careful."

"Don't forget," Troude went on, "the telephones don't work well at all and it's quite irksome not having any when they're out of order. Some need changing or, at the very least, fixing."

"In theory," said Miqueut, "I'm not saying you're wrong, there, but you can appreciate the costs that would be involved with that, given the fact, right ... in short, the simplest thing to do, you see, on the one hand, is to shorten the call, as much as possible, and, on the other hand, to call less often ... in such a way, in short, that everyone can get through.

"Would any of you like to raise anything else," he went on, "that we might consider in relation to this matter?"

"There's the issue of the secretaries ...," said Emmanuel.

"Ah, yes!" said Miqueut. "I was just coming to that."

Miqueut's outside line rang. He answered his phone.

"Hello?" he said. "Yes. Speaking. Ah! Director, Sir. It's you . . . My respects, Director, Sir."

With a wave of his hand, he begged his deputies' indulgence.

At the other end of the line, the Director was declaiming so loudly that it was possible for everyone to hear snippets of what he was saying: "some difficulty getting through to you . . ."

"Ah, Director, Sir!" Miqueut exclaimed. "I know full well! You see, the number of lines we have, currently, is quite insufficient, given our stature . . ."

He paused to listen.

"Precisely, Director, Sir," he continued. "It's because the N.C.S. has grown too quickly, as an institution, and yet, if I may be so bold, external support has not kept apace . . . We're suffering from growing pains . . . Ha ha!"

He began clucking like some hermaphrodite chicken who had swapped three cuttlefish bones for a basket of dates.

"Ha ha ha!" he continued, in response to the latest remark made by the Director. "You're absolutely right, Director, Sir."

" . . . "

"I'm listening, Director, Sir."

Thereafter, at regular intervals, he began proclaiming the words "Yes, Director, Sir," full of understanding, each time with a slight nod, doubtless out of deference, and while scratching his inner thigh with his left hand.

After an hour and seven minutes, he motioned to his deputies, indicating that they could leave, with a view to continuing the meeting later. Troude awoke with a start with a helping elbow from Emmanuel, and Miqueut was left on his own, holding the phone.

Occasionally, he would thrust his left hand into the drawer of his desk and pull out a cutlet, a biscuit, a slice of sausage, and various other foodstuffs that he nibbled as he listened . . .

CHAPTER XI

That afternoon, at five minutes to three, Antioch Tambrétambre got off his Kanibal and entered the Consortium building. On the seventh floor, René Vidal could hear the dull noise of the elevator's motor, which made the whole edifice shake. He readied himself to get up to receive his visitor.

Having reached the end of his quest, Antioch walked down the narrow corridor serving the offices on the seventh floor and stopped outside the second door on the left, which was numbered 19. There were only eleven rooms on that floor, but the room numbers started at 9, and no one had ever understood why.

He knocked, went in, and cordially shook hands with Vidal, to whom he felt drawn by an irresistible force of fondness.

"Hello!" said Vidal. "How are things?"

"Not bad, thanks," replied Antioch. "Is it possible to see Chief Junior Engineer Miqueut?"

"Wasn't the Major supposed to be with you?" asked Vidal.

"He was, but he lost his bottle at the last minute."

"He did the right thing," said Vidal.

"How come?"

"Because, since twenty-two minutes past nine this morning, Miqueut's been talking on the phone."

"Holy moly!" said Antioch, full of admiration. "Will he soon be finished?"

"We'll see!" said Vidal.

He went to the door communicating with the office of Victor and Levadoux.

Victor was on his own, writing.

"Is Levadoux not around?" asked Vidal.

"He's just left his office," said Léger. "I don't know where he is."

"Understood!" said Vidal. "Don't strain yourself on my account."

He returned to Antioch.

"Levadoux isn't in, so there's a slight chance that Miqueut will stop talking on the phone and ask to see him, but nothing could be less certain. I wouldn't want to lie to you."

"I'll wait fifteen minutes," said Antioch, "and then I'll leave."

"What's the rush?" asked Vidal. "You can stay with us."

"I am," said Antioch, "obliged, absolutely, to go and see my dentist, as I have an appointment."

"Monsieur likes pretty ties . . ." Vidal remarked, innocently, eyeing Antioch's neck, approvingly.

Antioch's silk tie was sky blue with little motifs in red and black.

"You said it!" Antioch conceded, blushing slightly.

They chatted for a few minutes more and then Antioch left.

Miqueut was still on the phone.

CHAPTER XII

Antioch returned for an update the following Monday, at around half past ten.

"Hey, buddy!" he exclaimed on entering René Vidal's office. "Oh, sorry! You're busy . . ."

Vidal, center-stage, at his desk, was presiding over the other five deputies.

"Come in, come!" said Vidal. "We're one short, as it happens!"

"I don't understand . . ." said Antioch. "Is Miqueut still on the phone?"

"Bang on!" clucked Léger.

"Which is why," Adolphe Troude piped up, "we're holding our own weekly meeting."

Levadoux, looking like Miqueut incarnate, took the floor.

"Today . . . Erm . . . I'm going to talk to you about something that seemed important enough for me to make it the subject of one of our little weekly meetings . . . It's the matter of telephones."

"Oh, no! Not again!" said Troude. "We're sick of it."

"Right!" said Vidal. "Rather than wasting time, let's cut to the chase: Will you join us for a drink?"

"I don't want to go out . . ." said Emmanuel.

"So, let's carry on being bored and bugging each other," said Léger.

"No. What would you say to a poetry competition?" suggested Vidal. "How about a limerick?"

"Fine. What's the first line?" asked Troude.

"There was a young man who said, 'Damn!'" declaimed Vidal.

"You didn't come up with that!" Léger asserted.

"How does it go?" Vidal insisted.

There was no answer.

"It's groovy . . ." he whispered, simply.

Victor blushed and scratched his mustache.

"Got any more?" asked Pigeon.

"Let me think . . ." said Vidal . . .

> If poor shoes you should put on your horse,
> Be aware, as you ride on your course,
> That the road will crack,
> As you race down the track:
> How will you get back, perforce?

"Approved, unanimously!" said Pigeon, thus summarizing, in two words, everyone's approval.

"Even so . . ." he continued, interrupting a five-minute silence, "I can't believe how bored we are . . . What d'you think, Levadoux?"

He turned round to where Levadoux had been sitting to find that he'd done a bunk.

CHAPTER XIII

At 4:00 p.m. on the 19th of June, exactly three months to the day after Antioch's second visit, Miqueut hung up.

He was happy as he had done a lot of good work and had succeeded in fine-tuning two draft circulars to be sent to the French Federation of Slope-Levelers regarding Camembert cheese rounds.

While he had been on the phone, the war had started, and with it the Occupation of France, which was something he could not yet worry about, given that he was unaware of it. Indeed, the invading forces had left the phone network in Paris intact.

N.C.S. HQ had also remained intact.

Miqueut's bosses, colleagues, and staff had all withdrawn to the provinces without worrying about him, as they knew he liked being the last one to leave work. For two days, now, they had been returning to work, in dribs and drabs, so Miqueut did not notice their temporary absence.

It was now time for the war to end, however, or, at least, for official hostilities to come to an end, because Miqueut, over the course of the last three months, had exhausted the provisions that had been stashed in his desk drawer, nibbling away at them mechanically, as was his wont.

Out of the entire workforce, only René Vidal had yet to return when, at 4:15 p.m., Miqueut opened the door between their offices. Vidal happened to be struggling up the stairs at that instant, because he'd had to walk some 275 miles back from Angoulême and was somewhat out of breath.

He entered his office the precise moment when Miqueut, having cast his eye all around the room, was about to close the communicating door.

"Hello, Monsieur," said Vidal, politely. "Are you well?"

"I'm very well, Vidal, thank you," said Miqueut, looking at his watch with the discretion of a gorilla. "Did your train get held up?"

In a flash, Vidal realized that Miqueut's phone call had lasted longer than planned. He went on the counterattack:

"There was a cow on the line," he explained.

"These train-workers are unbelievable!" said Miqueut, emphatically. "They could at least keep an eye on their livestock. Even so, it fails to explain why you're late. It's twenty past four and you're supposed to be here at half past one. A single cow . . . Really?"

"The cow wouldn't budge," said Vidal. "They're very stubborn animals, cows."

"Ah! That's true," said Miqueut. "Standardizing them would be no easy feat."

"The train had to go round the cow," said Vidal. "And that takes time."

"Understood!" said Miqueut. "And whilst we're on the subject, it seems to me that there could be a way of standardizing a system of rail tracks to avoid this sort of problem. Draw up a memo on that for me, would you . . .?"

"Absolutely, Monsieur."

Thereupon, having forgotten why he had come into Vidal's office, Miqueut went back to his pigsty.

Five minutes later, he opened the door again.

"I want you to understand, Vidal, that what I was pointing out, in terms of how important it is to be on time, was not so much for . . . you understand, as for reasons of discipline. We have to bend to discipline, and, vis-à-vis staff lower down, we must stick to a strict timetable; in short, you see, we must be very careful to be on time, especially at the moment, what with the rumors of war, and we who are more specifically predisposed to being leaders . . . in short, we, more than others, need to set an example . . ."

"Yes, Monsieur," said Vidal, with a sob in his voice. "I promise I won't let it happen again."

He was wondering who these "others" were and what Miqueut would say when he found out about the armistice.

After that, he went back to fabricating a Nothon project regarding council road-sweepers, with mustache, that he had not touched since he had gone off to fight in the pâtisseries of Angoulême. (He was too young and too green behind the ears to fight in the bars as his superior officers had done.)

In resuming this work, he took pains to include some obvious blunder that would need correcting on each page, which Miqueut would probably notice in the first hour's detailed inspection to which he would subject the project, and which would give him an excuse to go off on delightful tangents on the subject of appropriating terms from the French language for the thought that one wishes to express in the form of a sentence, and the consequences of this in relation, in particular, to the fine-tuning of a Nothon project.

CHAPTER XIV

A week went by and life at the Consortium began returning to normal. Chief Junior Engineer Miqueut had nine new bells fitted, one after the other, to the wall behind his chair to allow him—thanks to an ingenious system of combining the different timbres and frequencies of the bells—to summon each of the typists on that floor. The joy that this admirable apparatus gave him was immense.

In addition, it was at this time that he learned of the extraordinary events that had unraveled when he had been on the phone: the war, the Occupation, and the severe rationing. He showed no concern except, in hindsight, at having had his documents run the terrible dangers of pillage, plunder, fire, destruction, theft, rape, and massacre. His first move was to hide a toy gun in the door handle casing of his kitchen door and, from that moment on, saw himself fit to give his patriotic opinion on everything and anything.

While Miqueut would receive food parcels from the countryside, however, things were not going as perfectly for others. The cost of living had risen impossibly, and the typists under Miqueut's deputies, who were earning no more than 12,000 francs per month, and who were losing weight day by day, were all asking for a raise.

Miqueut therefore summoned the typists to his office, individually, with a view to giving them a little lecture.

"So . . ." he said to the first one, "it would seem that you're not happy with your wages. Will you get it into your head that the N.C.S. doesn't have the means to give you a raise?"

(The N.C.S. had recently been given a grant by the Disorghanisation Kommittees worth several million.)

"Will you also get it into your head," continued the Chief Junior Engineer, "that, proportionally, you earn more than I do?"

(This was true if one took into account the number of extra hours he spent wallowing in paperwork and initiating nits into matters of exegesis that some might describe as . . . debatable.)

"Why don't you just get married, anyway?" Miqueut went on, if the woman to whom he was talking happened to be a young maiden. "You'd soon see that you're earning quite enough."

(Since the day he'd gotten married, he'd saved money in lots of ways: his socks were darned for free, and he had nosh at home with no need for a domestic servant, which—tailor-maid—can be so difficult to find. The shortages caused by the war would allow him to wear his shoes down to the upper and to avoid washing without running the risk of being called a miser. In short, Miqueut had let himself go and appeared less and less as a good example of how to dress. He was saving up to buy a galvanized silver box in which to keep his Nothons.)

Having put the secretary at her ease, he would then spend a few minutes reeling off every mistake or blunder that she may have made since coming to work at the Consortium. Each item was exposed with meticulous scrutiny, after which he would eject the patient in tears and call the next one in.

As soon as he had expedited the lot of them and promised two out of twelve that they would receive the massive raise of at least 200 francs, Miqueut sat back in his chair, satisfied with himself, and set himself the task of examining a voluminous file to pass the time before his old enemy Touchebœuf would summon him to the Director General's office for the standard game of cards.

CHAPTER XV

As Miqueut would soon realize, to his detriment, there were many things that the war had turned upside down. Shorthand typists, attracted by premium wages offered by the Disorghanisation Kommittees, were thin on the ground, and would take only the most generous of job offers, as befits any commodity that is aware and apprised of its worth. These keyboard beauties now held their heads high, proud of being so necessary; and so, the day after Miqueut's outburst, eleven of the twelve scolded women resigned.

Miqueut grumbled about the ungrateful attitude of his underlings and made an urgent call to the Head of Personnel, Coffin. He was a graying character, ill-shaven, whose particular role—he was also the Director General's secretary—made him uncomfortable to handle.

"Hello?" said Miqueut. "It's Monsieur Miqueut. Is that Monsieur Coffin?"

"Hello, Monsieur Miqueut," said Monsieur Coffin.

"I need eleven secretaries, urgently! Apart from Madame Lougre, all of mine have left. Those that you chose must have been no good."

"Have you any idea why they decided to leave?"

"They didn't get on very well with my deputies and they never stopped arguing among themselves," lied Miqueut shamelessly.

Coffin, who was no fool, sighed like a Pacific steam train pulling out of the station.

"We'll try and find you some replacements," he said. "In the meantime, I'll send you some young ladies who've just joined the team."

What Coffin did, in fact, was send up to Miqueut the most average of shorthand typists because he wanted to keep the best for himself. More than that, he gave the following warning to the new arrivals:

"I'm going to assign you to a very interesting department, but . . . it's no easy job . . . It's Monsieur Miqueut's department. Of course, please understand, if you're not happy, don't just up and leave the Consortium. Rather, come and see me and I'll find another department for you."

None of this changed anything. Miqueut would have worn down a goat. He had previously caused the resignation of some thirty-seven secretaries in two months, and if the Director had not made his providential call, which had somewhat neutralized him, that figure would have been a lot higher.

The deputies decided to meet up in René Vidal's office.

"So . . ." said Vidal. "Are we on holiday?"

"How come?" asked Léger.

"We've no typists," Emmanuel explained.

"So what?" said Léger. "That doesn't stop us from working."

"It doesn't stop anything, including talking rubbish, from what I can see," Vidal remarked pleasantly.

"The only thing to do is to bunk off," said Levadoux.

"All the same," said Emmanuel. "It's crazy how boring it is, here."

"What would you expect?" said Vidal. "To be honest, it would be just as boring anywhere else, and we might not have such an easy ride. The only problem, here, is Miqueut."

"That's true!" chimed the other three in chorus. Léger was in the key of G, Emmanuel was in E, and Levadoux was in C sharp. Marion was asleep in his office and Adolphe Troude was with the Paper Committee.

The harmony of the scene was interrupted by the internal telephone.

"Hello?" said Vidal. "Hello, Mademoiselle Alliage ... Yes, please send him up."

"Hey, guys," he added, turning round to his colleagues. "I'm sorry, but I have a visitor."

It was Antioch Tambrétambre. Just five minutes before this, Miqueut had gone downstairs to play cards.

CHAPTER XVI

As he entered Vidal's office, Antioch was overwhelmed with emotion at the thought of finally getting to meet Miqueut. For the three previous months of war, he had fought alongside the Major. For eight days, just the two of them had defended a bar on the route d'Orléans. Barricaded in the cellar, armed with two colonial-era rifles and five cartridges—none of which would fit in the guns—they had held their position with prodigious courage, and not a single enemy soldier had managed to get to them. During that time, they drank everything the bar had in stock and didn't eat even a crumb. At no price would they surrender and nobody, moreover, would dare attack them. While this certainly facilitated their victory, their achievement was nonetheless brilliant, and had earned them the Military Cross with Palms. They wore their medals proudly, across the shoulder, and used the palm leaves to fan themselves.

Antioch and Vidal shook hands unreservedly, happy to see each other again after the horrors of war.

"How're things?" said Vidal.

"What about you?" replied Antioch.

They adopted an informal tone with each other quite naturally.

"Is Miqueut in?" asked Antioch.

"He's in a meeting . . ."

"May the coyotes of hell spit in his face!" bellowed Antioch, full of fury.

"They won't waste their saliva on that," was Vidal's opinion.

"Can you ask him again for a meeting?" said Antioch.

"With pleasure," said Vidal. "When for?"

"Next week, if possible . . . Or before then? But I daren't hope as much."

"Who knows?" said René Vidal.

CHAPTER XVII

Emmanuel had spent so long chasing the wild goose that morning that the poor bird had died of exhaustion. Its feathers were all over his office, and the carcass lay under Adolphe Troude's desk, which was covered with four tons of various fertilizers, all stored in little

BORIS VIAN

hessian sacks, as this commendable individual had a passion for growing vegetables in his garden, not far away, in Clamart.

Emmanuel consoled himself by feasting on a crust of bread. When he'd finished twiddling his thumbs, and other parts of his body, he made up his mind to knock on the door of his boss who, quite by chance, happened to be in.

"Enter," said Miqueut.

"May I speak with you for a minute?" asked Emmanuel.

"Why . . . be my guest, Monsieur Pigeon . . . Take a seat. I can devote at least four minutes to you . . ."

"I wish to ask you," said Emmanuel on entering, "if I might be authorized to take my holiday three days earlier than agreed."

"You're off 5 July?" asked Miqueut.

"Yes," replied Emmanuel, "but I wish to be off on the 2nd."

It was simply the sight of the dead goose that had given him the idea.

"Monsieur Pigeon," said Miqueut. "As you know, in principle, my only wish is to be able to give my staff satisfaction . . . However, in this instance, I fear that what you're asking of me may be somewhat difficult. It's not that, erm . . . you understand, I want, in any way, to prevent you from taking your holiday earlier than agreed . . . But now that the memo has been drawn up, I should like to know your reasons . . . in such a way that I might be able to see that they are valid . . . And not for a second do I doubt they are, but, as a matter of principle, right, it would be better for you to tell me."

"Monsieur Miqueut," said Emmanuel. "It's for personal reasons and it would be difficult for me to give you any details. Never have I hidden anything from you. However, in my opinion, it has nothing to do with work, and it would be completely futile for me to get swamped in explanations which would be of no interest whatsoever to you."

"Of course, my good Pigeon. I don't doubt it, but, you understand, what with the occupying authorities, we have to be very careful . . . At every point in time, we must be in a position to check that all staff are here, and you know that an acknowledgment of your absence such as that which would likely arise if you were to be off, as you're asking to be, several days before the given date, for reasons which are, of course . . . er . . . which are . . . er . . . excellent, but which . . . in short, are unknown to me . . . and which . . . that . . . well, you can see the drawbacks in not adhering to strict discipline. Speaking of which, moreover, you see, the same can be said for working hours . . . Please understand, I'm not referring to you, in particular, but in life, right, one has to be disciplined and punctual, and that is an absolute prerequisite for gaining the respect of staff beneath us, who, if . . . when . . . in cases such as . . . by chance, those when you were to be out of your office, would always tend to take things easy and, so you see, in short, as far as your holiday is concerned, it's a similar thing, and please understand that I'm not declining your request, but I am asking you to view this problem in light of these observations and, furthermore, are you up to date with your work?"

Silence.

For a whole hour on the clock, Emmanuel then said what was on his chest.

He said how much he hated always being upfront and only ever meeting people who were hypocrites, and that it had been exactly the same in his last job.

He said it was not in his nature to be enthusiastic or to lick people's boots either.

He said that he was used to saying what he thought and that if Miqueut was of the opinion that he was not doing enough, he just had to say so. He added, moreover, that he would not work any harder, if Miqueut were to tell him to, because he was already doing everything he could.

He kept saying what he was thinking, and Miqueut said nothing in response.

When Emmanuel had finally finished talking, Miqueut did reply. He said:

"In short, you're not wrong, in theory, but it just so happens that this year, precisely, I'm going to be off a bit earlier than planned, and I shan't be back before the 5th of July and, in short, you understand, it would be difficult for me to let you be off before I get back because you're the only one up to speed, right, with your jobs, and during my absence, someone up to speed needs to be here for the issue of nougat strainers, because, vis-à-vis external agencies, if someone were to telephone, the department must be able to give an answer, right . . . you see, in short . . ."

He gave him a big smile, patted him on the back, and sent him back to his office.

He did so because he was expecting Antioch Tambrétambre.

CHAPTER XVIII

Emmanuel was back in his office. He picked up his saxophone and produced a low B flat that reached a noise level of some 900 decibels.

Eventually, he stopped blowing, sure that his left lung had assumed the outline of the number 373.

He was just out. But only to the tune of one.

Miqueut opened the door and said:

"You understand, Monsieur Pigeon, as a rule, during working hours, er ... we must avoid ... er ... well, you see, in short. Anyway ... I wanted to ask you to draft a short memo for me, summarizing concisely ... er ... the meetings you might be having before I go on holiday ... giving a rough idea of the times you plan to have these meetings, a brief list of the individuals likely to be summoned, and the agendas to be discussed ... No details, of course, just a quick sketch of about twelve to fifteen pages per meeting will be plenty ... So, could you let me have that in ... half an hour, say? It'll take no time at all ... You should have it done in five minutes ... Of course," he added, speaking to Adolphe Troude, "I want the same from you and Marion."

"Of course, Sir," said Troude.

Pigeon said nothing.

Marion was asleep.

Miqueut shut the communicating door and settled back into his office.

Antioch had been waiting in Vidal's office for an hour and a quarter. The Major was with him.

Hearing Miqueut settle into his chair, they rushed out to the door in the corridor and knocked.

"Enter," said Miqueut.

CHAPTER XIX

Just as he was about to enter the Chief Junior Engineer's cage, Antioch collided with Adolphe Troude who, having torn out of his office as soon as Miqueut had left, was on his way back, buckling under the weight of an enormous brown sack. Antioch and the Major made room for him to get past, and Troude disappeared round the corner. Five seconds later, the building was shaken with a muffled thud.

Disturbed by this, the Major fled into Vidal's office, thus leaving his friend to meet his beloved's uncle on his own.

"Hello, Monsieur," said Miqueut, raising himself slightly from his chair and exhibiting a row of dull teeth through his grimacing smile.

"Hello, Monsieur," replied Antioch. "Are you well?"

"I am, thank you. And you?" said Miqueut. "My deputy, Monsieur Vidal, has informed me of your visit, but he's not told me exactly what it's regarding . . ."

"It's a rather unusual matter," said Antioch. "In a nutshell, here's what it's regarding. At a meeting . . ."

"Which panel do you represent?" Miqueut butted in, his curiosity piqued.

"You misunderstand," said Antioch, who was beginning to feel uncomfortable because of the smell in the room. It was causing him to lose his sang-froid, and his temples were awash with a moist fear. He pulled himself together and continued: "While at a 'surprise party' at my . . ."

"Let me stop you right there," said the mogul, "and allow myself to point out that, from a standardization perspective, the use of terms that have not been completely defined is unfortunate, and in any case, foreign terms should, as much as is possible, be prohibited. For this reason, we at the Consortium have been led to create special terminology committees whose job it is, in each field, to solve all these problems, which are very interesting, right, and which, in short, in each particular case, we take great pains to solve by covering ourselves, of course, with all possible safeguards, in such a way that, in short, we don't fall for flim-flam. Thus, in my opinion, it would be more advisable to use a term other than the English-sounding 'surprise party' ... and, what's more, by way of example, in this very organization, we typically use the French word *standardisation*, created to this end, and which is the preferred term, in the sense that ... er ... and not the English term 'standardization' which is used all too often, unfortunately, by those concerned and even by those who should, in short, make an effort to respect the rules of standardization unstintingly ... erm ... you see, as there is, in fact, a French word for it. It is always preferable to avoid using terms, the use of which may, in certain cases, prove unjustified."

"You are quite right, Monsieur," said Antioch. "And I share your opinion completely. But, as far as I can see, there is no French word that captures exactly the English compound of 'surprise party.'"

"I'll stop you right there!" said Miqueut. "It is not unknown, precisely, in the course of our work, for us to come across terms that are inappropriate or that are likely to cause confusion and give rise to different interpretations, depending on the term in question. We have several committees devoted to these problems, which are delicate in nature, it has to be said, and ... er ... you see, the solutions found are, generally speaking, satisfactory ... We have looked, for example, in the context of railways, which is as far removed from the present context as it could be, for an equivalent for the English word 'wagon,' used in French to refer to a 'carriage.' We organized a technical committee and, after a year's worth of research, which is not much if we consider that the paperwork, the meetings, and the public enquiry to which our Nothon projects are submitted lead to a significant reduction in the actual time it takes for jobs to get done, in short, we came up with the standardized French term *voiture* ... Well! You see, we've got the same problem here, and we could, I believe, solve it in the same way."

"You're right," said Antioch, "but ..."

"Of course," said Miqueut, "we are at your disposal should you require any information that may be of use to you regarding how our committees work. What's more, I'll have a Nothon information pack sent out to you, and you'll be able to see for yourself what ..."

"I'm sorry to interrupt," said Antioch, "but the matter I wished to discuss with you doesn't involve me in particular ... I'm here with a friend and, with your permission, I'll just go and get him ..."

"Go ahead, please!" said Miqueut. "So, it's your friend who'll draft the preliminary report on which our work can be built?"

Antioch made no reply and went to get the Major.

After the necessary courtesies, Miqueut carried on talking. This time, to the Major:

"Your friend has explained the reason for your visit, and I find your proposal extremely interesting. It will give us a series of Nothon projects that we'll be able to put before the appropriate committee in ... let's say, three weeks ... I think you should be able to get your first report to us in a week's time, and that would give us time, you see, to print the necessary copies ..."

"But ..." the Major began.

"You're right," said Miqueut. "However, to begin with, I think we should concentrate on the terminology, which is what any new report is based on ... The Nothon product will come later ... and that will give us time to have the necessary exchanges of opinion with those individuals likely to be affected by this project."

The internal telephone began ringing ...

"Hello . . ." said Miqueut. "Yes! But not now . . . I'm in a meeting . . . Oh! Really? Listen, it's quite inconvenient, but I can't . . . Yes . . . Right away . . ."

He cast over Antioch and the Major an eye filled with venom and reproach.

Having got the message, they rose as one.

"So, Monsieur," said Miqueut, becalmed, turning to the Major. "I'm very happy with this . . . er . . . first contact, and I hope, you see, that we can complete this report quite quickly . . . Looking forward to seeing you again, Monsieur . . . And goodbye, Monsieur," he said to Antioch. "Looking forward to seeing you again."

He accompanied them to the exit, rushed back for a pee, and then went off to find the Director General . . .

Antioch and the Major walked down the steps into the street and disappeared amidst the throng . . .

CHAPTER XX

At 31 rue Pradier, no birdsong rang from the toilets, no cricket crooned "The Trucker's Wife" in the background, no flower unfurled its multicolored fans to capture the foolish wingèd greenhorn, and even the mackintosh had folded away his tail, in eight unequal sections, with his lower jaw drooping down to the ground, and his eye sockets swimming with fat tears.

The Major was working on his Nothon project.

He was on his own, in his library, sitting on a summery lapis-lazuli rug, wearing handsome yellowy-orange apparel. His attire was in the typical Arab style, with all the trappings: he held a pipe hand-carved from bone, he donned a silken frockcoat, a compressor-style turban, and raw-deal sheep-leather sandals. With wild hair, and holding his chin in his right hand, he pondered, vigorously, the piles of various tomes stacked up on his table. There were as many as four volumes, all bound in leather from five-legged calves, and their dog-eared pages were testimony to the Major's veneration for the vivid memory of his grandfather, who, like a pig, would lick his finger and fold the tops of the pages over.

They were:

The Drunken Slave: A Manual by Joseph Dubonnet;

Considerations on the Grandeur and Decadence of the Romanians by Professor Rodica Stripov;

Five Weeks in Abalone by the Countess of Hanfrax, Laboratory Manager for the subsidiaries of Dugommier & Co., adapted by Jules Verne;

I, Chipmunk, or Losing the Habit, by Father Lewis.

The Major had never read these books before. Consequently, he was under the impression that they contained useful information, given that he knew the other two volumes in his library by heart—namely, the telephone directory, comprising two tomes, and his illustrated *Larousse* dictionary—and had not a clue as to what was truly original in them.

He had been working on the Nothon for eight days. And the problem regarding terminology had already been solved.

He was rewarded for his efforts by the dull pain he felt at the base of his cerebellum.

It was only fair. The full extent of his natural genius had been pressed into service.

As he spoke English fluently, it had not taken him long at all to observe that the one and only problem with the term "surprise party" for French-speakers was that it included the letter "y." After two hours of studying the question, the solution to the problem came to him in a flash: he replaced "party" with *partie*.

Matters of genius are rarely as simple as this, but when they do reach this level of simplicity, they truly define genius.

But the Major did not stop at that.

He passed from the general to the particular and considered the problem in terms of both space and time.

He researched the geographic aspects of venues that were most conducive to a good *surprise-partie*:

—the exposure of the site, including research into prevailing winds and geophysical constraints owing to altitude or to the granulometric composition of the soil.

He studied the architectural requirements for the building's construction:

—the different materials that can be used to build supporting walls;

—the types of anti-vomit and anti-macassar coverings needed for various surfaces;

—the ideal location for shaggoirs and parent evacuation points (if needed);

—hex hetera, hex hetera.

He extended his research to the tiniest of details.

Nor, moreover, did he fail to include relevant appendices.

Yet he was a little afraid.

But he did not despair.

He never despaired.

He preferred to sleep . . .

END OF PART II

PART III

The Major in the Hypoid

CHAPTER I

That morning, René Vidal had undone the second button of his blazer during the weekly meeting because it was so warm: indeed, the thermometer in Troude's office had just exploded, shattering three windowpanes and filling the room with a sulfureous odor. When the meeting was concluded, Miqueut motioned to Vidal— of all staff, as Shakespeare would say. He could very well have done without this, given the Beelzebubbling temperature in the lair of the Chief Junior Engineer, whose windows had all been scrupulously closed. Miqueut feared for his sensitive organs.

Vidal's colleagues left the room. Miqueut asked Vidal to take a seat and said:

"Vidal, I'm not happy with you."

"Oh?" said Vidal, who would gladly have stuck a fountain pen in the man's eye.

But the eye kept escaping.

"No! I told you, last year, when you rolled down the tops of your socks and wore a belt instead of braces, that, vis-à-vis outside agencies, we can't afford the slightest slip when it comes to the dress code."

"If something other than frog's blood ran through your veins," said Vidal, but not aloud, "you would feel the heat as much as I do."

"And can you please button up your jacket? You're not properly dressed, as you are. When you come into my office, I want you to take more care with how you look. It's a question of discipline. That's how we got to where we are today."

What Miqueut omitted to mention was the fact that discipline went completely out of his mind when it was necessary for everyone to respond to the alarm sirens. And their yelps could be heard at random intervals ringing over the rooftops.

He bored Vidal for a few more minutes with his extremely insightful thoughts on the importance of calculating the number of copies of a document that needed printing by thinking about the number of people due to receive a copy, as well as the levels of supplies in stock. As Miqueut had turned slightly to face him while lavishing him with such clarifications, Vidal wrought his revenge by drowning the toe of Miqueut's left shoe in sweat. When it had been reduced to the state of some gloopy stew (which is a defining feature of any good stew), Miqueut stopped talking.

Vidal left his boss, went back to his own office, and found the Major sitting at his desk, his legs stretched out and his feet resting comfortably on the telephone. A small puddle had formed under his left buttock, but Vidal only became aware of this when he got his seat back. The Major pulled up a different chair.

"I've recently had a cataract operation," he explained, "but they didn't get it all out and so, every now and again, it leaks a bit."

"How very agreeable it is," said Vidal, refreshed by the dampness with respect to matters fundamental. "What can I do for you?"

"I need some piping," said the Major.

"What for?"

"For my Nothon project looking at *Surprise-Parties*."

"What do you need?"

"Heating!" replied the Major, laconically. "I've researched everything, but left out heating. Not surprising, I suppose, what with the coal shortage and how hot the weather is. My subconscious must've deemed it superfluous."

He laughed at the idea of his subconscious.

"That's annoying," said Vidal. "I hope it doesn't screw everything up, at least . . . Did you look into refrigeration?"

"Damn, no," said the Major.

"Let's go and see Emmanuel, then," said Vidal.

In ten minutes, thanks to being so very competent in the field of refrigeration, Emmanuel had found a solution to the problem, which involved putting out the fire in the thingy with a good, cold shower.

"Did you leave anything else out?" asked Vidal.

"It's hard for me to tell . . ." said the Major. "Here . . . Have a look for yourself . . ."

He showed him his project, which ran to 1,500 pages in broadsheet format.

"I think that should do the trick . . ." said Vidal.

"I'm wondering whether Miqueut might notice that I left heating out. . . "

"He'll spot that at a glance," said Vidal.

"So I've got to finish the thing," said the Major. "Who's in charge of heating, here?"

"That'll be Levadoux," said Vidal, nervously.

"Oh, shit!" the Major sighed emphatically, but also with a hint of sadness.

Levadoux, of course, had done a bunk.

CHAPTER II

To replace the typists who had recently abandoned him, Miqueut had managed to get Coffin to recruit seven innocent damsels, whose merits, patently of the same order, roughly numbered zero.

Miqueut, only too glad at the prospect of showing these youngsters his idea of what makes a good boss, had a great time making them retype documents as many as eight or ten times in a row.

One thing he had not foreseen was the threat that would be posed to his overworked department by the National Junk Office's distribution of vitamin pills with added Cancoillotte cheese hormone and coated with wormcaster sugar. This super-energy confectionery had the most astounding effect on these young seventeen-to-twenty-year-old bodies. The slightest movement of one of these young women was filled with primitive zeal. After the fourth delivery of these pills, the temperature in their shared office had risen so drastically that any unsuspecting visitor, entering without taking special precautions, would be knocked sideways, almost keeling over from the inhuman energy of the ambient atmosphere. All one could do was run away or take one's clothes off very quickly to bear the heat but remain under no illusion as to anything happening thereafter.

The nucleolar body of the Chief Junior Engineer, however, with its constant supply of reptile blood, was impervious to this, like some salamander in fire, and his window remained shut, night and day, no matter what the air temperature was. To be on the safe side, just in case there should be a drop in temperature, Miqueut had even put on an extra cardigan as a precaution against any possible effects.

Sitting on a floral cretonne cushion on his chair, he was reading the shorthand transcription of a meeting when, suddenly, his eye ran into a short phrase that seemed harmless enough, but which jolted him so unpleasantly that he had to take off his glasses and rub his eyelids for six minutes, feeling no relief other than that afforded by a sting becoming a burn. He pivoted on his swivel chair and used a finger to press button number three in a complicated rhythm.

It was the secret code to summon Madame Balèze, his deputy secretary.

She came in. Her stomach, swollen with vitamin pills, stood out from a Tru-Tru Levantine dress with its pattern of large, petrol-yellow flowers.

"Madame," said Miqueut. "I am not at all happy with your shorthand. It seems to me that you ... er ... in short, that you may not have approached it with all due care and attention."

"But, Monsieur," Madame Balèze protested, "it seems to me that I've approached it with the same care and attention as usual."

"No," said Miqueut, incisively. "It's just not good enough. Look, on page 12, this is how you recorded what I said at that moment: 'If you envisage no problem with this, I think that we might, in line 11 of page 7 of document K-9-786 CNP-Q-R2675, replace the words "if applicable" with the words "unless otherwise specified," and add "and particularly in the event that" to the following line, for ease of comprehension.' Well, I never said that, I remember it perfectly well. What I suggested putting was 'if not otherwise specified,' which is completely different, and besides, rather than saying 'and particularly in the event that,' I said 'and especially in the event that,' which, as you can understand, is more nuanced. There are at least three mistakes of this magnitude in your shorthand, and things can't go on like this. What's more, before I know it, you'll be coming running to me, asking for a raise ..."

"But, Monsieur ..." Madame Balèze protested.

"You're all the same," Miqueut went on. "We give you *that* much and then you want more, as much as *that*. Try to avoid this happening again, or else I'll be in no position to offer the raise of 20 francs that I was thinking about giving you in a month's time."

Madame Balèze left his office without saying another word and got back to the typing pool just when the youngest woman in the department—who was given all the little jobs to do—had brought up the day's vitamin pills from downstairs.

Fifteen minutes later, the seven secretaries handed their notice in to Coffin and left the Consortium, en masse, to go and cheer themselves up with a little drink. Under their contract, they could not leave their position for good before the end of the month, and it was only the 27th.

So, they had a drink, paid the bar tab, and climbed back up the stairs to work.

They resumed their typing, and on account of their powerful fingers, the typewriters, one by one, were smashed to pieces. Yet again, the vitamin pills had wreaked their havoc. The carbon stencil papers, ripped by the third keystroke, were flying round the office in a cloud of overheated metal debris, and the smell of red correction fluid mingled with that of the enraged females. When all the typewriters were no longer usable, the seven secretaries sat down amidst the wreckage and started singing in chorus.

At that moment, Miqueut rang for his first secretary, the immovable Madame Lougre. She came running and informed him of the disaster that had befallen the office equipment. Miqueut scratched his teeth and, while he was at it, had a little bite at his fingernails, and then flew to see Touchebœuf so they could have a meeting about the matter.

Just as he was reaching the third floor, he felt a muffled bang which shook the whole building. The floor trembled beneath his feet. He lost balance and had to hold on to the banister to avoid falling, while an avalanche of joists, beams, and rubble came crashing down into the corridor that he had been about to enter, barely five meters away from where he stood.

Due to the weight of the sacks of fertilizer, Troude's office had just fallen through, taking with it an exceedingly interesting dossier containing a preliminary Nothon project regarding wooden crates for the transportation of Sudanese coconuts. It had taken three floors to halt the fall of the sacks of fertilizer, and Adolphe Troude, who had fallen into the bargain, was lying upright amidst the rubble. Only his head and his upper torso were sticking out from the debris.

Miqueut took twice five steps forward and looked in amazement at his deputy, who had lost his shirt and tie in all the mayhem.

"I have already reminded Vidal," he said, "of the need to pay great attention to the importance of being properly dressed. Vis-à-vis visitors, who can arrive at any time, we cannot allow ourselves, in the slightest, to overlook any ... er ... in short, of course, in the present circumstances ... you're not perhaps entirely ... well, right, in any case, just be very careful."

"It was a pigeon ..." Troude explained.

"What?" said Miqueut. "I don't follow you ... Can you express yourself more precisely?"

"It flew in," said Troude, "and landed on the electric light, which fell ..."

"I'll say it again ... That's no reason," Miqueut went on, "for neglecting how you dress. It's a question of correctness and respect for the person with whom you're talking. When rules are flouted, just look at where we end up. We are surrounded, alas, by far too many examples of this, and . . . erm . . . Well, in future, I think you'll take more care."

He turned on his heels, went back to the landing, and went into Touchebœuf's office, which was opposite the door to the lift.

Adolphe Troude managed to free himself and started gathering any sacks that had not split.

CHAPTER III

Despite the attempts made by Miqueut and Touchebœuf to get them to return to their better selves, the seven secretaries left three days later and never came back. They were in celebratory mood and did not even say farewell to the Chief Junior Engineer.

That day, at half past two, the Major had an appointment with his beloved's uncle.

As usual, the first thing he did when he got there was to go to see Vidal.

"And?" enquired Vidal.

"Ready!" the Major replied proudly. "The day before yesterday, I bumped into Levadoux at a bash and I asked him for some piping. Look . . ."

He showed him the project, which now ran to at least 1,800 pages.

"I hope you've followed the Nothon plan throughout, at least," said Vidal.

"Most definitely!" replied the Major, pleased with himself.

"Right. Go on, then," said Vidal, opening the door which separated his office from Miqueut's.

"Monsieur, Monsieur Lustalot is here to see you," he said to Miqueut.

"Ah, there you are, Monsieur Lustalot!" exclaimed the Chief Junior Engineer, rising from his chair. "I'm pleased to see you."

He shook Lustalot's hand for thirty seconds, with a grimacing smile splitting his chops.

Vidal caught no more of their conversation, as he closed the door and sat back down at his desk. He slept comfortably for an hour and a half and was woken by the sound of Miqueut's forced laughter seeping through the thin partition.

Discreetly, he went to the door to have a listen.

"You understand," his boss was saying, "it's very interesting work, but... er ... in short, you see, one shouldn't count on its being appreciated by everyone. In general, we end up running, and such is the case in almost all areas, into requirements of a somewhat commercial nature, as it were, against which we must endeavor to fight, but not, of course, by facing them head on, and demonstrate, you see, as far as is possible, as much diplomacy as we can possibly conjure up ... This work, in short, requires tact and no mean skill. And so it is, quite often, that we are met with arguments that seem to have been put to us in good faith. And yet! Three times out of four, we'll realize, further down the road . . ."

"When the Nothon has been approved?" suggested the Major.

"Ha ha! Fortunately, no," said Miqueut, with the voice of a man blushing. "Where was I? So, we realize that these arguments had been formulated from the perspective of purely individual interests. And often, you see, people can't avoid contradicting themselves, and they try to block us with reasons that don't hold up. That is why, in short, one must struggle ceaselessly to ensure that it is the perspective of standardization that triumphs.

"In short," Miqueut concluded, "our role is to be apostles and never give up."

"Be apostles . . ." said the Major. "Well! Why not?"

"That way, in no time at all," said Miqueut, "you'll see whether the job is suitable for you. I shall attempt to find a secretary for you. For the time being, I'm a little short of staff at that end of the scale . . . You see, it's very difficult to find junior staff, at the moment, and, in short, they're making such demands . . . well, we can scarcely allow ourselves to . . . you see, pay them more than they deserve. To do so would be to do them a great disservice. . . "

"Furthermore, I think," said the Major, "that in the initial stages, I should concentrate on getting up to speed."

"Indeed, you see, in short, you're exactly right, in part . . . and besides that, the Head of Personnel has promised me seven typists in about a week's time. As there are already six deputies under me, I don't think you'll have a typist straightaway, because I need one in addition to Madame Lougre, who's the only loyal one among them, but I . . . er, thereafter, I think we'll be able . . . to complement one another, you see . . . Moreover, I have it in mind . . . I've a niece, who's quite good at shorthand . . . in short, I have it in mind to employ her in the department . . . she'd be appointed to you . . ."

Vidal heard a strange little noise, like the hiccup of a public schoolboy, followed by a crash of someone falling to the parquet floor. The door opened almost immediately.

"Vidal," said his boss. "Help me move him . . . He's had a funny turn . . . probably on account of fatigue caused by drafting the project . . . Anyway, his document seems very interesting . . . Your office is the place for that."

"The project?" asked Vidal, as if he had not understood what he meant.

"No, no, no," said Miqueut, roaring with laughter . . . "Monsieur Lustalot! He's joining the N.C.S."

"You managed to persuade him," said Vidal, doing his best to make it sound admiring.

"Yes," Miqueut confessed, full of false modesty. "I'm thinking of giving him the Special Committee for *Surprise-Parties* which is due to be created imminently."

Meanwhile, the Major had managed to get up by himself.

"Forgive me," he said. "It's fatigue."

"Don't mention it, Monsieur Lustalot . . . I hope you're feeling much better now. Well! So then, I look forward and so on . . . See you next Monday."

"I look forward to it," repeated the Major, struggling internally to use such language.

Miqueut went back into his office.

CHAPTER IV

Fromental, meanwhile, was not dead.

He'd had his Debrieka repaired—which is to say he'd had a car fitted to the steering wheel which had taken him home after the party. This new configuration was more practical when it came to driving friends around.

He'd joined the Racing Club de France rugby team and had been training hard in order to build an impressive pair of biceps with which to smash the Major's face in at the first available opportunity.

Through the rugby club, he had become friends with André Vautravers, Secretary General to the Delegation ... Chance is a funny old thing...

He'd also started hanging out with the infamous Claude Abadie, shameless swimmer and basketball player, as well as amateur jazz clarinettist.

Such was the extent of his friendship with Vautravers that, not content with seeing him at rugby training, he obtained through his intervention a position with the Delegation ... In this way, he was to oversee the Consortium's activities, to some degree.

Fromental took up office a week before the Major went to see Miqueut. His work consisted, purely and simply, of filing the documents issued by the N.C.S. for the purpose of filling piles and piles of hefty folders.

Fromental had set about his work with enthusiasm. And in some dark corner of his cerebral lobes wriggled a diabolical little thought.

He would flatter Miqueut and compliment him on the excellent quality of his work, and so, little by little, get into his good books. That accomplished, he would bring out the big guns and ask him for his niece's hand in marriage. The plan was simple but effective, and made easier to achieve by the number of meetings that he would surely have with the Chief Junior Engineer.

Three weeks to the day after starting work with the Delegation, Fromental received the Nothon project for *Surprise-Parties* that had been put together by the Major.

Little knowing this, and in view of the exceptional importance of the document, he drafted a letter to Miqueut in which he acknowledged receipt of the project and included glowing words of praise for its author.

His draft letter was approved without amendment, because his boss had been very busy with his secretary, and so the missive went out to the next link in the chain.

To make matters worse, Fromental picked up the telephone.

He dialed the well-known number, MIL.00-00, by some miracle got through to the receptionist, and asked for Monsieur Miqueut.

"He's not in," replied the female switchboard operator (who was the only pleasant person working there). "Would you like to speak with one of his deputies? What is it regarding?"

"Surprise-parties," Fromental answered.

"I see. In that case, I can put you through to the Major."

A noise like the cussing of a tinker with his wife resonated inside Fromental's head, and even before he had time to wonder whether the Major in question was *his* Major, he had him at the other end of the line.

"Hello?" said the Major. "Your friendly neighborhood Major, here."

"It's Vercoquin, here . . ." he blurted out, giving himself away in his confusion.

On hearing these words, the Major let rip into the mouthpiece a scream that was carefully calculated to perforate three-quarters of the right tympanum belonging to Fromental, who dropped the receiver and, groaning, held his head with both hands.

When the wretch picked up the telephone again, the Major continued:

"I'm sorry," he said with a snigger. "There's something wrong with my phone. In what way may I be of service to you?"

"I wished to speak with Chief Junior Engineer Miqueut," said Fromental. "Not with one of his deputies."

Riled by this, the deputy in question spat into the mouthpiece of his telephone, and Fromental's left ear was immediately blocked by a thick liquid. The Major then hung up.

Fromental also hung up. Using a twisted paperclip with a cellulose swab at one end, he cleared his blocked ear passage with great difficulty.

It took two hours for the storm booming around his parietal lobes to calm down. Having regained the ability to think, he set about drawing up a detailed schedule of various ways in which he could possibly make trouble for the Major and so cause Miqueut to come to hate him.

He knew the Major's ineffable charm only too well to not doubt for a minute that the Major would achieve his aim, which was to get Miqueut to like him, provided that favorable circumstances or the absence of unfavorable circumstances were to leave the way open for him to do so.

What he had to do, therefore, was to counterattack. And *presto*.

Vercoquin locked his desk drawers, got up, carefully pushed his swivel chair up against his desk (simply to give himself time to think) and left his office without his right glove.

He went downstairs. His Debrieka, for which he had managed to obtain a valid Occupation parking permit, was waiting patiently for him on the pavement.

He had—by dint of such cunning and craftiness!—discovered Zizanie's address. He started the engine, put the car in gear, and set off at full speed for where the beauty lived.

At 5:00 in the afternoon, having parked outside her house, he began his watch. At 5:49 precisely, he saw her return home.

He started his engine up again, drove forward for 4.2 meters so as to be exactly opposite the building's porte-cochere, and stopped again.

Seven times he took the Lord's name in vain because he was hungry, thirsty, and needed to pee, but he remained at the wheel, his eyes glued to the door.

He was waiting for something.

CHAPTER V

At 7:30 in the morning, he was still waiting. His left eye was stuck shut with fatigue. He managed to open it with a pair of combination pliers and once more found himself endowed with the ability to see properly.

He stretched his numb legs out so strenuously that they went through the floor of the Debrieka's footwell. As the car was not exactly free of the need for repairs, he paid it no attention.

A quarter of an hour went by and then Zizanie came out. She was riding a lovely war-issue dogwood bicycle. The tires were made from vipers' guts inflated with acetylene, and the seat was a thick layer of low-fat Gruyère that was quite comfortable and practically indestructible. Her light skirt fluttered behind her, revealing her little white knickers with a short, chestnut-colored fringe at the top of her thighs.

Slowly, Fromental followed Zizanie.

She took rue du Cherche-Midi, turned onto rue du Bac, followed rue La Boétie to boulevard Barbès, went up avenue de Tokio, and reached place Pigalle directly. The Consortium stood not far from there, behind the École Militaire.

Guessing where Zizanie was heading, Fromental accelerated sharply and reached the N.C.S. two minutes before she did. That gave him just the time he needed to race to the bottom of the stairs and call the elevator, which was at the second underground level.

Zizanie, who had not spotted him, walked sedately toward the makeshift bike shelter and carefully tied her bicycle to one of the steel supports holding up the corrugated iron roof. She took her bag. When she reached the cage of the elevator mechanism, which served only the two upper floors, by order of decrees in force, she pressed the call button.

From below, Fromental prevented the elevator from moving by holding the door open. As a result, it did not budge.

"A power outage!" thought Zizanie.

She then set out by foot to climb the six times twenty-two steps leading to her uncle's department.

She had just begun heading up to the fifth floor when the elevator rattled into action. It reached the seventh floor the very instant she was to set foot at the top of the stairs. Opening the elevator's forged iron door, seizing Zizanie, pulling her into the elevator, and pressing the button to go down was all child's play for Fromental, whose passion, clearly visible under the delicate fabric of his summer trousers, heightened the vigor of his movements, even if it also somewhat impeded the natural ease with which they were executed.

The elevator came to a halt when it reached the ground floor. Having released her during the lift's descent, Fromental seized Zizanie once more and opened the internal folding door from right to left. The external door opened automatically, as the Major had just turned up.

Swiftly, with his right hand, the Major pulled Zizanie into his arms. With his left, he extricated Fromental from the lift and threw him down the stairs to the basement. Then, followed by Zizanie, he calmly entered the elevator, which soon delivered them to the seventh floor.

In the time it took to go up six floors, he'd had time enough to do good work. But on exiting the lift he slipped on said work and nearly broke his nose on the stone floor of the landing. Zizanie just caught him in time.

"You saved me as well, my angel! We're even," said the Major, kissing her tenderly on the lips.

She was wearing a very greasy red lipstick which left its mark on his face. Before the Major was able to erase the compromising smears, Miqueut, who was on his way down to see Touchebœuf, suddenly loomed from the corridor and stood before them.

"Ah! Hello there, Monsieur Lustalot . . . So! I see you came at the same time as my niece . . . Allow me to introduce you to your secretary . . . Hmm . . . Hmm . . ." Turning to Zizanie, he continued, "Get to work. Madame Lougre will tell you what needs doing." Intently eyeing the Major's mouth, the loquacious man enquired, "Have you been eating strawberries? It's a bit early in the season, I'd have thought . . ."

"There are plenty in my garden," the Major explained.

"You're lucky . . . Hmm . . . Hmm . . . I'm off down to see Touchebœuf. Do what you can to get up to speed until, in short, we get an opportunity to have a little meeting . . . to get an overview of the situation."

As these social pleasantries were being exchanged, the elevator had gone down again. It was now on its way back up, bringing with it a Fromental full of fury. When he saw Miqueut, he was quite taken aback.

"Hello, my good man," said Miqueut, who had first met him under the auspices of the Delegation. "So … What's new? I'm guessing you were coming to fetch me for the meeting with Touchebœuf?"

"Er … That's right!" Fromental faltered, seizing gratefully on the pretext provided.

"By the way, allow me to introduce Monsieur Lustalot, my new deputy," said Miqueut. "Monsieur Vercoquin, of the Delegation … It was Monsieur Lustalot who drafted the Nothon project on which the Delegation so kindly congratulated us," Miqueut added.

On repeating the words "the Delegation" in quick succession, Miqueut was sick to the back teeth: he could barely breathe.

Fromental muttered something that could have been interpreted however one wanted. What the Major heard and what Miqueut heard were quite different things.

"Well," Miqueut interjected. "let's take that elevator, my dear Vercoquin, given that it's here. See you later, Monsieur Lustalot."

The Major was highly amused as they disappeared from his sight.

On entering the corridor on the seventh floor, the Major burst out laughing in his characteristically fiendish manner, and nearly caused the secretary under Vincent, an engineer in Touchebœuf's department, to faint: she was a lanky, graying old bat who saw herself as the object of sexual harassment at every turn …

CHAPTER VI

The Major settled himself comfortably in Vidal's vast office, as the latter was off doing a tour of the seventh floor somewhere. The Major was already up to speed with the institution's routines and had learned, in particular, that when Miqueut headed downstairs, it was a green light for his deputies to go on walkabout.

He picked up the telephone and dialed 24.

"Hello? Monsieur Lustalot, here. Can you put me through to Miss Zizanie, please?"

"Of course, Monsieur," a woman's voice replied.

A minute later, Zizanie was in his office.

"Let's go down and have a Himalaya," the Major suggested.

Not far from the Consortium there was a milk bar where you could consume an array of very cold things, swimming in various juices that were quite exquisite and had extravagant, highfalutin names.

"But . . . What about my uncle!?" Zizanie objected.

"To hell with him," the Major replied, coldly. "Let's go."

They did not, however, leave immediately. Pigeon and Vidal came in and discreetly looked away to give the Major time to button up. As soon as Zizanie was ready in turn, they joined them, as they were thirsty as well.

"And so?" Vidal enquired as they slowly went down the stairs. "First impressions?"

"Excellent," said the Major as he tidied himself up.

"That's great," said Emmanuel, who indeed seemed open to being favorably impressed by Zizanie's charms.

As soon as they got outside, they bore left (not the Major's left) and went down a passage protected from the fall of various meteors by safety glass with an embedded netting of soldered metal wires making up a square mesh that was 12.5 mm thick, give or take the odd micrometer. It was the preferred route of Vidal and Pigeon, who wished to avoid any encounter either fortuitous or unforeseen, or even unpleasant or possible, with individuals likely to surface from the metro, and who might, moreover, work with the Consortium, and who might hold a position that would allow them, down the line, to cause all sorts of trouble for these two interesting characters. Furthermore, it had the advantage of making the journey longer.

There were bookshops galore in the passage, and this secondary advantage served only to increase the appeal of this secret route.

At the milk bar, a fairly attractive strawberry-blonde waitress fixed them four bowls of ice cream. And that's when Emmanuel spotted André Vautravers. They were old classmates, having been in the same year when studying for the See-Pee-Hey exam.

"How are you, old pal?" Vautravers cried.

"And how are you?" Pigeon replied. "Wait. Don't answer that. I can tell from looking at you that you're doing well."

Vautravers, it is true, was wearing a magnificent new suit and light suede shoes.

"It's well-paid work at the Delegation," Emmanuel went on.

"It's not bad," admitted Vautravers. "What about you? How much are you earning?"

In hushed tones, Emmanuel gave him the number.

"My dear friend," bellowed Vautravers, "that's peanuts . . . Listen to me, I hold enough sway at the Delegation these days to be able to ensure that Requin will get you a raise. All he'd have to do is give the nod to your Director-General . . . Easy-peasy . . . You see, for us to be treated so differently is just unacceptable . . ."

"Thanks, old pal," said Emmanuel. "Can I get you a drink?"

"No, thanks. I'm sorry but I've got to meet up with some mates, and I'm already late ... Bye, everyone."

"Well," said the Major, when Vautravers had left. "He seems like an interesting person to know ..."

"Quite interesting," Emmanuel agreed.

"Sorry to trouble you," Vidal interjected, "but could we, perhaps, get a move on, because ..."

"There's a chance Miqueut will be on his way up soon," the Major finished.

"No, that's not it," said Vidal. "I'd quite like to have a browse round my favorite bookshop."

CHAPTER VII

The Major had been working in Miqueut's department for a month already and his love life had made little progress. He did not dare speak with the uncle about his feelings for his niece.

All that the aforementioned uncle could think about was the first meeting of the General Committee for Surprise-Parties, which had been convened to go over the Major's Nothon project.

Everything was ready.

All the carbon copies, duly checked, had been printed and stapled.

All the illustrations had been designed, as Miqueut would have expressed it, "to facilitate full and accurate understanding of the project's provisions."

A hundred and fifty invitations had been sent out well in advance, with the expectation that nine people would attend.

An idiot-proof guide to the agenda had been frantically drafted by the Major for the Head of the Committee.

Said head was none other than Professor Epaminondas Lavertu, member of the Institute, and famous the world over for his research into the impact of Saturday-night binge-drinking on the reproductive capacity of assembly-line workers.

The department under Madame Triquet, who was responsible for organizing any meetings, had long been on the ball, and its offices were brimming with signage and notices that were to be used to direct people to the meeting room, kindly provided, for this occasion, by the Paris division of the Union of Ticketless Jam-Makers.

An hour before the meeting was due to start, the Major was bouncing up and down the corridors and stairs like a goat, checking everything, collecting files, going through documents so as to be able to answer any potential questions, and generally ensuring that nothing was out of order.

When he got back to his office, he had barely ten minutes to get ready. He quickly changed his shirt, substituted his light-rimmed glasses for a dark pince-nez made from tooled Bakelite that looked more distinguished, and grabbed a notepad for making a detailed record of the meeting.

While it was true that Chief Junior Engineer Léon-Charles Miqueut insisted that a full record of discussions be taken in shorthand, as a rule he forbade his deputies, whose job it was to draft the minutes, from using the shorthand record, which took several days to translate and resulted in voluminous sheaves of paper that nobody would ever look at again.

The Major took a quick peek to see if his boss was in his office but saw that he had gone downstairs. Then he remembered that the

Director General was due to attend the meeting: on such occasions, Miqueut and Touchebœuf would spend a good while beforehand explaining what he should avoid saying. Indeed, there were often times when the Director, carried away by the speaker's passion and enthusiasm, would come out with ideas that were so sensible that the Committee would purely and simply reject the Nothon projects being reviewed.

Without waiting for Miqueut, the Major therefore went straight to the meeting room. Zizanie was already there. It was her job to take the shorthand notes of the meeting.

A few members of the Committee were already scattered around the table. Others were hanging their hats on the pegs in the cloakroom, while exchanging profound observations on the issues of the day. The only people who ever came to these meetings were old hands who all knew each other.

Enter the Director General, followed by Miqueut, sniffing, head to wind, that sweet meeting smell. As they came in, the Major was honored by a handshake and was introduced, in quick succession, to Chairman Lavertu and a few lesser characters.

Of the hundred and forty-nine people invited to the meeting, twenty-four were present, and the Director General, seeing this unprecedented success, was rubbing his hands in delight.

Government Delegate Requin, accompanied by Vercoquin, made his entrance, both carrying sober, leather briefcases. Chief Junior Engineer Miqueut, falling over himself with groveling, left the latter to his own devices and escorted the former to the rostrum.

In the middle, the Chairman. To his right, the Government Delegate and the Director General. To his left, Miqueut, then the Major.

Vercoquin lurked somewhere in the room, but he had not managed to get anywhere near Zizanie.

One of the typists passed round an attendance sheet for everyone to sign. The faint hubbub of scraping chairs and inscrutable murmuring died down to silence, and the Chairman, with one eye on the idiot-proof agenda given to him by the Major, opened the meeting.

"Gentlemen. Today's meeting brings us together to examine, before it is sent, potentially, before a Public Hearing, a Nothon draft proposal relating to surprise-parties, a copy of which, I believe, you have all received. This document has struck me as very interesting, and so, before we begin, I shall ask Monsieur Miqueut to explain, better than I ever could, the manner in which this meeting will proceed and ... er ... its aims ..."

Miqueut hawked loudly to clear his throat.

"So ... Gentlemen, you see ... This is the first time that the Committee for Surprise-Parties has convened and you have all been so good as to be party to it ..."

"With no pun intended," the Director General interrupted, guffawing.

The Committee discreetly showed its appreciation for this witty comment, after which Miqueut continued:

"May I therefore remind you ... er ... that this Committee was inaugurated at the behest of various stakeholders and by the agreement of the Central Government Delegate, Monsieur Requin, who has graced this first meeting with his presence ... And, to begin with, let us share with you the names of the members of this Committee."

He motioned to the Major, who, having learned it by rote, reeled off the list of the hundred and forty-nine members of the Committee at one go.

This feat made a great impression on those present and the atmosphere in the room began to glow with a quite particular sparkle.

"Would the Committee like to make any suggestions at all, or have any modifications to recommend, regarding this list?" Miqueut continued, seamlessly, in as formal a style as he could muster.

Nobody replied and so he carried on.

"Gentlemen . . . Before examining document s-p-1, I shall, you see . . . er . . . for, in short, and specifically, those individuals not aware of how we go about things, the procedure followed by the Consortium when processing a new Nothon."

In broad terms, and in his own inimitable style, Miqueut explained the committee's *modus operandi*. Five individuals, including one General Inspector, who had somehow sneaked into the meeting unseen, abruptly fell asleep.

When he finally stopped talking, the Committee's ears were ringing with absolute silence.

"And so, gentlemen," Miqueut went on, relying on his trusty exordium, "with your permission, let us proceed to examine the document . . . er . . . which is the focus of this meeting."

At this point in time, Vercoquin rose discreetly from his chair and whispered something into the ear of the Government Delegate, who nodded in agreement.

"I should like to suggest," said the Delegate, "that the person who drafted this important research read it out to us. Who is the author of this work, Monsieur Miqueut?"

Perturbed, Miqueut replied only with a muffled grunt.

"May I remind you," said the Director General, seizing on the opportunity to wheel out a long-winded speech that he knew all too well, "that under the terms of the provisional order of the fifth of November nineteen-wotsit-and-one, the development of Nothon draft proposals falls either to the Standardization Bureau under the auspices of each Professional Committee, or to those researchers appointed by the N.C.S.'s Technical Committees, and their creation and composition are submitted for approval from the appropriate State Secretary."

By now, everyone else at the meeting, all half-asleep or nodding off, had given up trying to follow what was being said.

"And may I, in turn, remind everyone," said Fromental, having signaled his desire to speak by raising a hand, "that, under no circumstances, may the members or engineers of the Consortium stand in the stead of the aforementioned Technical Committees."

So malignant was the gaze he directed at the whole of the Major's person that the Bakelite frame of his pince-nez instantly corroded in three places. Caught in the flak, the tip of Zizanie's pencil snapped clean off.

Miqueut's slender temples were covered in a cold, ill-smelling sweat. The situation was critical.

The Major then stood up. He cast his bi-monocular gaze round the assembled company, and addressed them in these terms:

"Gentlemen. I am the Major. I am an engineer with the N.C.S. and the author of proposal S-P-I."

Fromental was jubilant.

"Proposal S-P-I," the Major continued, "is a significant work."

"That is not the issue," interjected Requin, annoyed by such waffle.

"And yet," the Major went on . . .

"Firstly, when I began this work, I was not yet an engineer with the N.C.S. The account of the appointment I had with Monsieur Miqueut, appended to the S-P file, attests to this.

"Secondly, in the development of this project, I was assisted by an agent for manufacturers and consumers, who, in order to take part in this, organized a number of surprise-parties. While on a limited scale, the Technical Committee was, therefore, an appropriately constituent part of this work.

"Thirdly, may I respectfully point out to the Government Delegate that proposal s-p-1 was drafted in accordance with the framework provided for Nothons."

The Government Delegate's eyes were ablaze.

"How interesting!" he said. "Let me see . . ."

He immersed himself in reading the weighty document. Great sighs of hope filled Miqueut's lungs, only to escape from his half-open mouth in the form of hovering wisps.

"This work," said the Delegate, looking up, "seems perfect to me and abides, in all aspects, by the framework provided for Nothons."

The members of the Committee, with thousand-yard stares, were motionless, gripped as they were by the charm distilled from the Major's soft voice.

The atmosphere in the room thickened and began to split into misshapen, slightly rippled slivers.

"Given the lack of comment thereon," said the Delegate, "I think, Monsieur Chairman, that we may send this proposal before a Public Hearing, unaltered. And not least because the way it is organized, in line with the Nothon model, makes it very easy to read."

So sharply did Fromental bite his lower lip that it bled like a Vietnamese potbellied pig.

"Dear Government Delegate," concluded Monsieur Lavertu, in a hurry to get back to his girlfriend who was in a jazz bar, "I am in complete agreement with you and I see that we have reached the end of the agenda. Gentlemen, it remains only for me to thank you for your attention in this matter. The meeting is hereby adjourned."

The word "adjourned" echoed round the meeting room and had the magical result, given the favorable conditions in which it worked, of waking the General Inspectors.

The Government Delegate had stayed behind and was having a word with Miqueut.

"This is an excellent draft, Monsieur Miqueut. You had something of a hand in this, I believe . . ."

"Goodness!" cried Miqueut, with a humble smile, which was less dangerous as it meant that his teeth remained unseen. "It was drafted by my deputy, Monsieur Lustalot . . . in short . . ."

Having narrowly escaped, his confidence came back.

"Ah, I see," said the Government Delegate. "You're always so modest, Monsieur Miqueut . . . I'm sorry I raised that matter, back there, in the meeting, not least because there was no substance to it, but I receive so many documents that I never have time to read them, and the advice that I got from Vercoquin—who has only just joined us and who is, understandably, somewhat overenthusiastic, and can therefore be forgiven—had seemed . . . well, that's all in the past, now. Goodbye, Monsieur Miqueut."

"Goodbye, Monsieur, I look forward, er . . . and I thank you for being so kind . . ." said Miqueut, with his nose in the air. He was shaking Requin's hand like a leaf, as the Government Delegate tried to leave the room, with Fromental, ashen faced, following him. "Goodbye, Monsieur, I look forward to, er . . . Goodbye, Monsieur . . . Goodbye, Monsieur . . ."

The meeting room emptied slowly. The Major waited until everyone had left, then followed his boss up to the seventh floor.

CHAPTER VIII

"He looked awful, didn't he?" said Zizanie, with a whiff of pity in her voice.

It was the afternoon of the same day. The Major and his darling were in Miqueut's lair, as he had just gone downstairs to play cards. The Major was buzzing with excitement. He had won the battle and planned to benefit from that. From his point of view, all the signs led him to believe that Miqueut, by hook or by crook, would be able to see his merits. For now, therefore, Fromental was of little importance to him.

"He got what he deserved!" he said. "That'll teach him, the bellicated she-shnuff, to come looking for a fight with me!"

The Hindustani expressions with which he peppered his speech were, for Zizanie, an inexhaustible source of delight.

"Don't be so harsh, my love," she said. "You should make up with him. After all, he does have a parking permit."

"So do I," said the Major. "And I have a lot more money than he does."

"That makes no difference," said Zizanie. "This is all so upsetting. Deep down, he's good-natured enough."

"How do you know?" said the Major. "Alright! I don't want to refuse you that. I'll invite him to eat with us, this very afternoon. Does that make you happy?"

"But it's three o'clock . . . And you've already eaten."

"Precisely!" the Major pronounced. "We'll soon see if he's of a mind to be friends."

Fromental accepted the invitation, over the phone, without hesitation. He too was keen to prick the boil.

The Major told him to meet him at his usual milk bar at half past three. They both arrived at the same time, at four o'clock.

"Two of your most expensive triple Himalayas!" the Major ordered, producing his ration book and the money to pay for them.

Fromental wanted to pay his way, but the Major cut him short with a fiery stare. Sparks of electricity jumped from the tiled floor to his left hand, and he wiped his brow with a silk handkerchief.

They sat on the tall, faux-leather barstools and began tucking into their ice cream.

"I think it would be better if we cut the formalities," said the Major, off the cuff. "What have you been up to, this afternoon?"

The question took Fromental aback.

"None of your business!" he replied.

"Quit the tough-guy act," the Major went on, twisting Fromental's left wrist with consummate skill. "Go on, tell me."

Fromental let out a shrill scream. When he realized that everyone was looking at him, he tried to pass it off as a coughing fit.

"I've been writing poetry," he eventually confessed.

"D'you enjoy that?" the Major asked, surprised.

"I love it ..." he whimpered, lifting his eyes to the ceiling, seemingly in ecstasy, while his Adam's apple bounced up and down like some Russian dancer.

"Do you like this?" the Major asked, and he began to recite:

The uneasy breezes slurred their antiphony
To the uncanny jerks of the corpse from the West ...

"Incredible!" cried Fromental, who started to weep.

"You'd not heard that one?" asked the Major.

"No!" Fromental exclaimed with a sob. "The only poetry I've ever read was in some random volume by Verhaeren."

"That's all?" asked the Major.

"I never even thought about the possibility of there being others . . ." Fromental confessed. "I'm not inquisitive and I lack initiative, but I hate you . . . You took my love away from me . . ."

"Show me what you came up with earlier!" the Major ordered him.

Timidly, Fromental produced a sheet of paper from his pocket.

"Read!" the Major commanded.

"I daren't!"

"I'll read it myself, then!" said the Major, and he began, with his wonderfully resonant voice, to read it out:

PHENOMENAL INTENTIONS

At his desk, the man sat writing,
Hurriedly, but with sterile rage.
Sat writing, and the spider of his quill
With still words spun enough to fill the page.

When, unraveled, the page was filled,
Bang! With his finger, he pressed the button.
Gaping door, hunter there. Bizarre! . . . A cap?
Quick! Telegram! Twenty francs, son.

Two legs went up and down, pitter-patter,
Like the feet of a squirrel. Pedaling . . .
Brakes. Counter. Fill in form. He leaves.
Twenty francs up, he was. Came back at a saunter.

And the telegraph wire, mile upon mile,
It went up, it went down, as did those feet,
Following the train tracks, but horizontally,
As feet do not.

Miles and miles of telegraph wire,
Stuffed, completely, with words getting held up
Where the wires are attached, from pole to pole.
Pray may they keep standing.

Two hundred thousand miles . . .
Covered in just one second? Come off it!
Indeed, were it not for all these coils,
All these coils, these wretched pitfalls for words.

At his desk, the man, pleased and relieved,
With a cigar betwixt his teeth,
Sat reading the Sunday supplement.

Miles and miles of telegraph wire,
And inductors, in which words, lost,
Twisted and writhed like damned souls
In some living hell, or like mice
Trapped in the old blue enameled iron jug . . .

At his desk, he sat finishing his cigar,
Pleased and relieved, for within hours
He would have word from sweet Dudule.

"Not bad," said the Major, after a short silence. "But you're being influenced by the poets you've read. Well, the poet you've read . . . One volume by Verhaeren . . ."

They were both quite unaware of the commotion being caused by the milk bar waitresses, who had all gathered behind the counter to hear them more clearly.

"You write poetry as well?" asked Fromental. "I can't tell you how much I hate you!"

He nervously twisted his tibias together.

"Not so fast!" said the Major. "Listen to this . . ." And he began to recite:

I

In turquoise suede shoes and a beret basque,
Harmaniac the drunkard drank from his flask
Sweet absinthe, wallowing in life corrupt,
Nonstop, night and day, he fucked and he supped.

Born in the South, where the grapes of France grow,
And sun-cooked garlic perfumes the air so,
A poet he was, good-looking perchance,
So worked not and lived on rue de Provence.

His body being tuned by five skillful whores,
To heady heights of stardom his mind soars,
As he writes his verse in sleazy places
Full of snotty noses, stupid faces.

Come the night, his balls would bulge like udders,
Yet find release in glorious shudders.
Like a randy racehorse on Spanish fly,
He'd come first, twelve times, then leave on a high.

II

Alas, the green ghost with festering sores
Came knocking, one night, checking all the doors.
The pale-faced pox caught up with him shagging
With three lovely lasses, hot and gagging.

The more passionate one's sport, vice, or likes,
The greater the torment when the pox strikes.[†]
Harmaniac, devoured by horny ghosts' fangs,
Suffered terrible pain, atrocious pangs.

He wandered the streets, having lost his mind,
Then Tabes dorsalis *his limbs confined.*
Crippled so cruelly, aphasic, inane,
Yet a spark of hope, for some, did remain . . .

The pox might be cured! So, medical teams
Looked after him and covered him in creams.
They sterilized modern tools and drains
To extract the vile poison from his veins.

....

† Professor Marcadet-Balagny, Clinical Studies.

BORIS VIAN

The voiceless words into worms mutated,
Immured through being unarticulated
By the poet, pinned down, as in a vice.
But still, they would out, no matter the price.

Alive with dactyls, a sticky morass,
Crawling with anapests, writhing en masse,
Spondees and trochees, the vengeful clew grew . . .
Squirming, word-worms, a spreading retinue,

Teemed from the thalamus to skull's hard wall.
In an orgy, they formed a deadly ball,
Each armed with a sword, unsheathed from its chape,
They slashed through the membrane, as if a grape.

IV

Harmaniac held on. Under such attack
A writer of prose would fail to fight back.
But the poet, shaped by heavenly hand,
Is built to survive without a brain. And

The doctors still pumped his veins with the cure,
But the worms, relentless, hungry for war,
Merely grew, and grew, until . . . filled with heat
Inhuman, his body did in defeat

Go stiff and then stuck, as if in a brace.
All reeled on seeing the look on his face,
Blaming spirochetes for his sad demise.
Someone went to the corpse, to close his eyes,

And placed a soft hand on his chest. The shock!
"His heart beats still!" he said, lifting the smock . . .
And there reared the head, so sticky with clart,
Of the filthy dark worm munching his heart . . .

The Major had gradually lowered his voice in order to emphasize the horror of the final verse. Fromental was rolling around on the floor, sobbing. One by one, the waitresses had fainted like skittles, but luckily, there were few customers at that time of day. Summoned by the Major, it took just two ambulances to carry all the victims away.

"You shouldn't!" groaned Fromental, flat on his belly in the sawdust and holding his head in both hands.

He was drooling like a slug.

The Major, also somewhat overcome with emotion, helped his rival get up.

"Do you still hate me?" he asked him in a quiet voice.

"You're my mæstro!" said Fromental as he placed his cupped hands on the top of his head and bowed, an unmistakable sign of veneration in India.

"You've lived in India?" asked the Major, on seeing this strange maneuver.

"I have," replied Fromental. "When I was very young."

The Major felt his heart swell with love for the far-ranging wanderer who, with him, had so many passions in common.

"I like your poetry as well," he told him. "Let us be brothers rather than rivals."

He had found that line in an old almanac.

Fromental got up and the two men kissed each other on the forehead as a mark of affection.

They then left the milk bar, carefully closing the door behind them as there was not a living soul left in the room. In passing, the Major gave the key to the woman selling sandwiches outside who, born deaf, had survived unscathed.

CHAPTER IX

Toward the end of the evening, the Major was slowly climbing his way up to Miqueut's office.

On his instruction, Vidal and Emmanuel had cut the phone wires, thus ensuring that he would not be disturbed for as long as it would take. And so, for a full thirty minutes, Miqueut had not moved a muscle.

The Major reached Miqueut's door, stood tall, knocked, and in the blink of an eye, went in.

"I should like to ask you something, Monsieur," he said.

"Come in, come in, Monsieur Lustalot. You're in luck, the phone's been a bit quiet for a while."

"It's about this morning's meeting," said the Major, swallowing a hiccup of laughter on hearing Miqueut's words.

"Ah! Yes . . . Actually, I should congratulate you . . . You had, in short, prepared rather well for the meeting . . ."

"In a word," said the Major, "I saved your bacon."

"May I remind you, Monsieur Lustalot, say . . . that, as a rule, a certain deference is expected regarding . . ."

"Indeed," the Major interrupted. "But let's face it; without me, you were up the creek."

"It's true," Miqueut admitted, taken aback.

"It's a fact," expanded the Major.

Miqueut said nothing.

"My reward!" roared the Major.

"What do you mean? You want a raise? But you'll have it, of course, my dear Lustalot, when the three months of your probation are up ... I'll see to it that you are rewarded, say, as much as the means of the Consortium, which are somewhat meagre, will allow ..."

"That's not what I mean!" said the Major. "I wish to have the hand of your niece in marriage."

"?...?...?..."

"Yes. I love her, she loves me, she wants me, I want her, and we are getting married."

"You're getting married?" said Miqueut. "They're getting married ..." he added, out loud, to himself, flabbergasted. "But what's any of that got to do with me?"

"You're her guardian," said the Major.

"In principle, that's quite correct," he agreed. "But, say, er ... in short, it seems to me that you're rushing things somewhat ... As far as your work is concerned, things won't be easy ... It will mean you're absent ... for at least twenty-four hours ... And with the amount of work we have to deal with, at the moment ... You'd have to organize it so that you get it done and dusted in a morning ... or an afternoon ... Getting married on a Saturday afternoon would be perfect, say, because, in short, that way, you wouldn't have to take any time off work ..."

"Of course," the Major agreed, having no intention whatsoever of ever setting foot in the N.C.S. again after getting married.

"But, in short, my niece would carry on working here as a secretary, right?" said Miqueut with a winning smile. "If not, I can see another way round this . . . She could stay at home and, to keep busy, without payment, obviously, given that we should no longer be her employer, she could type up your papers, without, in short, having to leave the homestead . . . Hmm . . . Hmm . . . And that would keep her busy . . ."

"That would save a lot of money," said the Major.

"Right, then. I'm behind you, one hundred percent . . . Carry on, as you were . . . You have *carte blanche.*"

"Thank you, Monsieur," said Lustalot as he left the room.

"So, I'll see you tomorrow, my fine Lustalot," concluded Miqueut, holding out a sweaty palm.

CHAPTER X

Their engagement was announced by the boss to his deputies a few days later. Before informing the others, Miqueut told Vidal and Pigeon the news, because he had to give them Zizanie's invitation to the little event organized for this purpose.

Thus he summoned Vidal into his office and said:

"My dear Vidal, I'd like you to know that . . . er . . . at my niece's request . . . we . . . the family would be happy to welcome you from seven o'clock on the evening of the engagement party . . ."

"But Lustalot had told me to be there at four."

"That's right, as a rule, it will start at four, but, personally, I don't think it will be much fun before seven . . . This sort of party, as you know, is . . . er . . . isn't, in short, very interesting . . . So, my advice to you is to not turn up too early . . . and you wouldn't want it to interfere with your work . . ."

"That's something that must certainly be taken into consideration," said Vidal. "With your consent, I'll turn up at five o'clock and I'll ask the Consortium to take an hour and a quarter off my monthly salary."

"In that case," said Miqueut, "I believe that would be perfect, of course . . . You'll just have to make up for lost time on a Saturday afternoon . . ."

"Why, of course," said Vidal. "And it goes without saying that it would be completely pointless to pay me for the overtime . . . After all, we're not even paid by the hour."

"How right you are! We must be apostles. Do you have anything urgent for me? What about your meetings? Is everything fine?"

"Yes," said Vidal. "Everything's fine."

"In which case, I thank you."

Miqueut, alone for a second, used the internal phone, which had been repaired, to call Pigeon.

Emmanuel duly appeared.

"Please, take a seat," said Miqueut. "Now then . . . er . . . I've multiple things to tell you. Firstly, I can tell you that my niece has invited you to her engagement ceremony, from seven in the evening next Wednesday at her home. Just have a word with Vidal, who's been invited as well, and sort yourselves out workwise."

"Lustalot had told me to be there at four . . ." said Pigeon.

"Yes, but, look, we've got the Nothon project regarding metal tins for boiled sweets to finish off before then. Will you manage that?"

"I think so," said Emmanuel. "If need be, I could always come into work earlier."

"That would be an excellent solution. What's more, as a rule, there's nothing stopping you, when you have a lot of work on, from coming in earlier, every day . . . You see, our work here is akin to that of an apostle, and if one day, as I wish it may be, we see the creation of a golden book of the benefactors, in short, of our great Consortium, it should include the biography of all those who, right, will have sacrificed, as you yourself just suggested you do, their pleasure on the altar of Standardization. What's more, that's no mere supposition and it could be perfectly positive. Moreover, I'll make a point of discussing this very soon with the Delegate. At any rate, I very much like your suggestion of doing overtime, because it shows me that you take your work seriously. Speaking of which, I've some good news for you. Do you remember what I told you a few months ago? I said I'd look after you at the N.C.S. Well, by dint of interventions made on my part to the Director General, I've managed to get you a raise, starting this month."

"Vautravers has done a good job," Emmanuel thought to himself. Then, aloud, he said:

"I thank you, Monsieur."

"You see, at the moment," said Miqueut, "what with the difficulties we're having, I think two hundred francs per month is not to be sniffed at . . ."

Pigeon, liberated shortly thereafter, began roaming up and down the corridors under a cloud of impotent rage. He burst into the office of Levadoux and Léger.

Wonder of wonders: Levadoux was in. Léger was not.

"You not done a bunk?" asked Emmanuel.

"I can't. That cretin Léger's just phoned me to say he can't get here anytime soon."

"How come?"

"He's come to blows with the cashier of his dad's factories. It turns out the bugger's gone and nicked two square decimeters of prewar rubber that Victor was using to plug holes in the cages he keeps ants in."

"What does he want it for?"

"For putting new soles on his shoes!" said Levadoux. "With rubber! When there's no shortage of wood. It's incredible!"

"But why are you making such a fuss?"

"What? For once, Miqueut is due to bunk off at four, as my notepad and spy will testify, and I've got an appointment at a quarter past three to see my, er . . . little sister! If only Léger were here to tell people that I'd just left the office . . ."

Pigeon left the office, laughing hysterically, and disappeared down the corridor.

A good distance from there, Léger was rolling around in sawdust with an old man with a funny little beard, and viciously biting his right shoulder.

Levadoux was back at the ranch, on call.

CHAPTER XI

On the day of the engagement party, Pigeon and Vidal put in an appearance at the office at half past two in the afternoon, looking as resplendent as stars in the night sky.

Pigeon was wearing a light-colored suit in a seductive shade of bluey gray. His yellow shoes had a honeycomb of holes on the top and soles on the bottom. The white shirt that he was wearing was immaculate and his tie had broad diagonal stripes of sky blue and pearl gray.

Vidal was sporting his sea-blue Zazou suit over a turtleneck top. It was painful to behold, as it made him look like he had accidentally squeezed his head into a tube that was too narrow.

The typists nearly fainted when they saw them, and Victor, whose father had been high up in the fire brigade, in charge of men with a certain *savoir-faire*, had to quickly massage their chests to get them breathing normally again. When he had finished his good work, his face was a shade of saffron and his mustache stood stiff.

Vidal and Emmanuel pretended to work for an hour and then met up in the corridor, raring to go.

As they left, they bumped into Vincent, who just happened to be wearing his Sunday best—a suit cut from an old sack for charcoal. So as not to spoil it, he had substituted the jacket for an old gas-engine filter made from the finest cotton, with holes cut in it for the arms. As was his wont, he was pushing his little belly out. He had brown hair, which was thinning and, with a laudable sense of harmony, allowed his scalp to gradually take on the same color. To stave off boredom during the long winter evenings, he used his face as a breeding ground for a profusion of green scabs which he enjoyed scratching with his black fingernails. His plan was to use his skill to scratch out a map of Europe on his face, and he scrupulously ensured that it was always up to date.

Cautiously, Vidal and Emmanuel shook hands with him and then promptly left the building.

Zizanie lived in a fine apartment, chaperoned by some old, penniless female relation who acted as her housekeeper.

She was not short of money or of aged, distant cousins, all of whom had wasted no time in accepting her invitation. Also among the throng were to be found the fruits of Miqueut's line, altogether a respectable number of these indistinct individuals that young people typically refer to, generally, as "relatives."

As far as young people are concerned, parties involving "relatives" are always dead in the water. Zizanie's party was no exception to this rule.

The mothers present, starting with the premise that young people "dance in such an amusing manner," did not take their eyes off their daughters for a second and formed an almost impenetrable wall around the group of youngsters. A few brave couples, personal friends of Zizanie's (probably orphans) tentatively dared some second-rate swing moves. No sooner had they started than they had to stop because the circle of relatives' heads closed in on them so that they owed their survival only to an energetic escape involving lashing out with their feet. Despondent, they retreated to the record player. The buffet was inaccessible, besieged as it was by a tight crowd of "decent people" wearing dark suits, voraciously scoffing the spread put on by Zizanie and staring angrily at any youngsters rude enough to dare help themselves to a tiny cake. Woe betide the unfortunate Zazou who managed to get his hands on a glass of champagne. He would be manipulated by such refined maneuvering as is used in the oil industry in the direction of some horrible old bint caked in makeup who would take the glass from his hand in exchange for a syrupy smile. As soon as the plates full of canapés were brought out, they were annihilated by the extraordinarily dangerous characters that are the cousins in their frock coats. Little by little, the "relatives" expanded and the youngsters—crushed, constricted, suppressed, and reduced to nothing—found themselves crammed into the furthermost corners of the apartment.

A friend of the Major's, Dumolard junior, managed to get into a small lounge which happened to be empty. Delighted with this, and throwing caution to the wind, he began an elegant swing with a young girl in a short skirt. They were joined by two more couples, who found their way in without the relatives noticing. They all thought they'd found a haven, but it wasn't long before the worried expression of one of the dancers' mothers appeared at the door. In the blink of an eye, each and every seat in the lounge was creaking under the weight of keen-eyed women wearing a benevolent smile which killed the swing music resonating from the room next door and turned it into a pitiful Boston one-step.

From time to time, Antioch, dressed in a black suit (chosen deliberately for this purpose), approached the buffet—always at a slight angle so as to make himself look older—and managed to obtain enough comestibles to avoid keeling over from starvation. Thanks to his sea-blue suit, Vidal was also doing quite well on this front, but Emmanuel and the Zazous were relentlessly driven back.

Trapped in a group of old bints plying her with poisonous compliments, Zizanie had little by little begun to capitulate.

Miqueut had squeezed behind the buffet, where the maître d's were standing, doubtless for surveillance purposes. His little rabbit jaws worked away without respite. Every now and again, he would put his hand in his pocket, move it to his mouth, pretend to cough, and then started chomping again. In this way, he could take food from the buffet less often. He simply had to fill his pockets every hour or so. He took little interest in the people around him: the Commissioner was not there. And there was nobody from whom to request a Nothon project.

As for the Major, he was alone in a corner.

The Major was getting the whole picture.

The Major was suffering.

Emmanuel, Vidal, and Antioch were suffering from watching the Major suffer.

And the party went on amid the baskets of lilies and Gabonese pernambuckles with which the Major had lavishly decorated the rooms.

Slowly, all of the little Zazous and Zazoutes disappeared down the mouse holes, because the decent people were hungry.

The maître d's were carting out cases of champagne by the dozen, but the champagne always seemed to evaporate before getting anywhere near Zizanie's friends, who were now shrinking like dehydrated vegetables.

At this point, the Major flashed a secret sign to Antioch. He, in turn, had a quiet word with Vidal and Pigeon, and the four of them headed for the bathroom.

Emmanuel remained outside to keep watch.

It was 5:52 p.m.

CHAPTER XII

Full as a flagon and looking even more pernickety than usual, if that was even possible, Miqueut picked up his white rayon scarf, his black overcoat, and his black hat, at 5:53 p.m. With briefcase in hand, he took "English leave" and faded away. Leaving his wife where she was and continuing to chew little morsels of cake, he was heading for the N.C.S.

At 5:59 p.m., Emmanuel, hailed by a male voice, went into the bathroom. He surfaced at 6:05 p.m. and set about discreetly closing the apartment's exterior doors.

At 6:11 p.m., the Major himself came out of the bathroom, only to return, seconds later, followed by six stocky Zazous.

The six guys in turn came out of the bathroom at 6:13 p.m. and began, in accordance with the *modus operandi*, to mingle with the people at the party.

The Major made sure that Zizanie was safe by locking her in the bathroom.

At 6:22 p.m., the operation was set in motion.

The individual in charge of the record player switched it off and hid the records.

Then six Zazous, having removed their jackets and rolled up their sleeves past the elbow, advanced in one line toward the buffet, each of them armed with a solid oak kitchen chair. On the Major's command, the six chairs crash-landed with a dull thud on the front line of frock-coated men who had chosen to imagine that these quickly deployed maneuvers were simply some stupid prank on the part of the youngsters.

Three men fell to the ground, knocked out. Another, with a little beard and a gold chain, started guffawing like a goat, and was immediately taken prisoner. Two others picked themselves up and ran off, routed, to the maître d's.

Wielded with better aim, the same chairs were used to bring down the whole of the second line.

The auxiliary Zazous were not idly twiddling their thumbs. Seizing the old bints, they marched them to the kitchen where, turning them upside-down, they sprinkled their secret beards with Cayenne pepper, much to the displeasure of the spiders.

The frock-coated men were utterly routed in a matter of mere minutes. There was no attempt at resistance at all. The prisoners, having had their hair shaved off and their faces daubed with boot polish, were thrown down the stairs. The females ran off, hell for leather, in search of a bucket of cold water in which to sit.

There were not many dead, so they fit easily in the dustbins.

After that, the Major went to look for Zizanie. Standing in the middle of the chaotic battlefield, with one arm around his partner's shoulder, he rallied his valiant troops.

"My friends!" he cried. "We have endured a tough battle. And we have triumphed. Thus perish the pesky. But now is not a time for words. It is a time for action. We cannot stay here in this pandemonium. Gather any food supplies you can find and let us press on for a surprise party."

"Let's go to my uncle's house!" a pretty brunette suggested. "He's away. Only the servants are there."

"Away on holiday?" asked the Major.

"He's in the dustbin," she replied. "And my aunt only gets back from Bordeaux tomorrow night."

"Perfect. Come, gentlemen. To work. Two men to carry the record player. One for the records. Ten for the champagne. Twelve girls for the cakes. Everybody else, bring ice and the bottles of booze. You've got five minutes."

Five minutes later, the last Zazou was leaving Zizanie's apartment. He was buckling under the weight of an enormous block of ice which had begun to melt and was dripping down his neck.

Antioch made sure the door was secure.

The Major led his troops from the front. By his side walked Zizanie. Behind him, his major seconds (ha ha!).

"To the uncle's house!" he shouted.

He looked back, one last time, and the eager company set off boldly down the boulevard.

The rearguard, carrying the ice, was sopping wet . . .

END OF PART III

PART IV

Passion for Jitterbugs

CHAPTER I

The uncle's apartment was on avenue Mozart, on the third floor of a luxurious building of Comblanchien limestone. It was tastefully furnished with exotic trinkets brought back from some distant expedition to the heart of the Mongolian savannah. Deep-pile carpets from the Merovingian period, shorn (as per cats), absorbed the reactions of the nervous embossed oak floor. Every detail conspired to produce the overall effect of a cozy, comfortable home.

When the concierge saw the Major's battalion approaching, she dug herself into her little shelter. The niece, Odilonne Duveau—by any other name she would still smell as sweet—bravely entered this nest of resistance and engaged the concierge in trenchant negotiations. Slipping a five and zwantzig note into the discussion soon smoothed the corners of the exchange, which concluded with an impressive march up the thick carpet of the stone stairs.

The procession came to a halt outside the door of Odilonne's uncle's abode, whereupon the aforementioned niece inserted the phallic aluminum-bronze rod into the keyhole which lay waiting. Through the variously alternating and combined action of loaded springs and opposing forces, the bolt began playing the great aria from *Aïda*, as desired. The door opened. The cortège jerked forward once more, and the last Zazou, now empty-handed as the ice had all melted, carefully closed and locked the door behind him.

Antioch issued a few quick instructions and the effect of his genius for organization was such that some six or so minutes later all the equipment and supplies were in their place.

Even more than that, cognac by the caseload was found in the uncle's supplies. Its discovery plunged the Major into unadulterated rapture, and the seventy-two extra bottles were added to the rest of the provisions brought back from Zizanie's.

The faceless crowd of Zazous set to work on the rooms, rolling away rugs, moving furniture, emptying cigarette packets into handier pockets, and getting ready to dance.

The Major gathered his bride-to-be, Antioch, Vidal, and Pigeon for an urgent council of war.

"Stage one of our operation is complete. It remains only for us to give this event the brilliant sheen it rightfully deserves. Any ideas?"

"Let's phone Levadoux and tell him to come and join us," Emmanuel suggested.

"We can try!" said Vidal.

"That's peripheral," interjected the Major. "Rather, Vidal, get on the phone to the Hot Club and get us a band. They'll make more noise than the record-player . . ."

"Waste of time!" said Vidal. "We need Claude Abadie."

He seized the telephone and dialed the well-known number: Molyneux, thri-ate-toe-too.

While Vidal made his call, the Major continued his speech.

"For this to be a success, we need two things: First, we have to get them to eat, so the drink doesn't make them ill. Second, we have to get them to drink, to make them happy."

"I'll make sure they eat," said Zizanie. "I need a few girls, willing and able," she shouted as she headed to the kitchen, soon to be followed by the number of helping hands desired.

"Abadie's on his way," Vidal reported. "Gruyer's going to drop by my place to pick up my trumpet."

"Right," said the Major. "Now, let's phone Levadoux."

"It's a bit late," Vidal replied.

The prehistoric cuckoo clock announced the time as twenty to seven.

"You never know," said Emmanuel. "Let's try anyway."

Luckily, the Consortium's switchboard operator, having been held up by Miqueut, was still there.

"Monsieur Levadoux has left," she said. "But leave your number with me . . . If he comes back this evening, he'll call you back."

She laughed at her own little joke.

Emmanuel gave his number, which she duly noted next to his name on a piece of paper.

"If I see him on my way home, I'll tell him to give you a call," she promised. "Would you like me to put you through to Monsieur Miqueut?"

"Thanks, but no thanks," said Emmanuel, quickly hanging up.

There was no chance on earth that Levadoux would return to his office that evening, and so the operator bumped into him on the stairs as he was heading to fetch his gloves, which he'd left on his desk when he'd left for his See-Pee-Hey exam.

She informed him of Emmanuel's message, and Levadoux came knocking on Odilonne's uncle's door some thirty minutes later.

Followed to the letter, the Major's instructions had already begun to yield good results. A number of Zazoutes were carrying around trays that formed the base of pyramidal piles of ham sandwiches (or pyramygdal hams, as ear-nose-and-throat specialists call them). Others were covering tables with plates of cream cakes. The Major, hiding behind an immaculate tablecloth, was mixing his favorite tipple: a Monkey Gland with red pepper.

From a hook in the larder ceiling there hung, stripped of meat, the ham bone. Around this, five males (plainly) were executing a fierce dance. The rhythm of this wild whirl was beaten out by the muffled banging of the cook, Berthe Planche, who had been locked in a cupboard. When she started losing the beat, they took her out of the cupboard and all five of them violated her, two at a time. They then put her back in the cupboard, only this time on the lower shelf.

And, lo! The Commotion of Abadie's Jazz Group was heard at the front door. On hearing this, Zizanie rushed to let them in.

CHAPTER II

"Where's D'Haudyt?" asked Vidal, when the door had been opened.

"He's just taken a little tumble down the stairs with his drum-kit!" Abadie replied, his ear ever listening for bum notes.

"Let's wait for him."

When they were all together, the group made their entrance and were greeted by the applause of the great crowd of their admirers.

"We can't play in the living room if the piano's in the library," Abadie shrewdly commented. He'd certainly wasted no time studying at the Ecole Polytechnique. "Come on, guys. Bring the piano in," he ordered four Zazous who were standing idly by in a corner, twiddling their tom-toms.

Eager to make themselves useful, they rushed to the piano, a super-size Pleyel weighing 1,500 pounds, including the pianist.

The doorway was too narrow, and the piano refused to jump over the threshold.

"Turn it round!" ordered Antioch, who knew a thing or two about ballistics. "It'll go through sideways."

In executing this maneuver, the piano lost only its cover, two legs, and seventeen tiny pieces of marquetry, eight of which would end up broken by the time the piano was delivered.

The piano was reaching its destination when Abadie appeared once more.

"Come to think of it," he said, "I reckon we'd be better off playing in the library. The acoustics, as they say in Savile Row, are better suited."

As the piano was still on its side, finishing the job was quite easy. The broken legs were replaced with piles of big books taken from the shelves of the uncle's collection. It worked just fine.

"Hey, guys. I reckon we can get going, now," said Claude Abadie. "Tune up."

"Come and have something to cool you down before you start playing!" the Major suggested.

"I won't say no!" Claude replied.

While his bandmates were drinking, Gruyer, a lecherous twinkle in his glasses and his hair untamed, was taking the opportunity to renew contact with a female medical student he knew, more or less. His nostrils were quivering, and his flies were bulging.

He was stopped, on the slippery slope of vice, by the voice of his band leader, summoning him to the hubbub.

In only ten minutes, the Major had poured a hundred liters of fiery beverages down the parched throats of the throng.

Among the first to take advantage of this unending supply was Peter Gna, the famous romantic. Having had four glasses of orangeade filled to the brim with brandy, he was beginning to feel in the mood. His nostrils flared, he breezed around the room, and then disappeared behind a curtain hiding a window and settled himself comfortably on the balcony.

Abadie was playing his big hit: "On est sur les roses." The Zazous were happy as could be. Their legs twisted like wishbone ocarinas while their wooden soles beat a strong 4/4 rhythm, which, as André Cœuroy would put it, is the very soul of Negro music. And he knows as much about music as Henri Rousseau knows about history. The languorous lowing of the trombone lent the dancers' gyrations an almost sexual aspect, and seemed to issue from the throat of a salacious bull. Pubic regions rubbed vigorously against each other, doubtless so as to wear away those growths of hair which are so irritating when itching oneself and likely to contain little scraps of food, which is disgusting. Full of grace, Abadie was standing at the front of the band, and every eleventh beat, he would let forth an aggressive grunt by way of syncopation. The atmosphere perfectly encouraged a crazy tempo and so the band were giving it their all, just about managing to play like thirty-seventh-rate Black jazzmen. Chorus followed chorus, but no two choruses sounded at all the same.

The doorbell rang. It was a gendarme. He complained that he had been hit on the head by a falling bronze planter weighing approximately ninety-three pounds. The matter was investigated, and it was found to be a dispatch from Peter Gna, who was beginning to wake up on the balcony.

"It's an outrage!" the gendarme grumbled. "A Ming dynasty planter! What a vandal!"

His fractured skull prevented him from dancing as well as he might have, and so he didn't stay for long. He was offered cognac, which he drank with pleasure. Then he wiped his mustache and dropped dead down the stairs.

Abadie was now playing another of his old hits, "Lay By, Goody" by George Crapp-Swynge. On noticing this, the Major poured himself two glasses of brandy.

"Good health, Major!" he said graciously, clinking the glasses together. He drank the second one first to be polite, then drank the first. After this, with a view to overseeing the smooth running of proceedings, he set off down the corridor . . .

On the large table in the dining room, he noticed atop two muscly legs a downy derrière trembling amidst two more slender legs, smooth and covered in some brownish dye (The gravy's a fine and private place . . .). It was dark in the room, so he could not see exactly what was going on.

"Stay in cover!" he said kindly, regardless, for he could see that the young woman was preparing to pull away.

Discreetly, he headed back down the corridor.

The Major had a good ear and had become aware, over the last few bars, that the intensity of the music had decreased markedly. The only possible cause for this could be that Gruyer had stopped playing. Richer for having acquired caution by experience, he opened the door of the next room with great care.

In the closed-curtain gloom, the Major could make out a silhouette with a frizzy mop of hair and glistening glasses, whom he identified immediately. A lighter silhouette, becomingly plump, was lying on a nearby couch, having shed all superfluous clothing. A curse, which had been a long time in coming, greeted the Major as he entered, and left the room as he carefully closed the door behind him.

Undaunted, the Major set off, once more.

He bumped into Lhuttaire, who played clarrrinet with vibrrrattto, and who had just located (and pocketed) a decanter. The Major informed him in a whisper that it would be worth his while to pay a routine visit to Gruyer's lair as the latter would not take long, once his initial emotion was assuaged, to swing into action. Lhuttaire nodded his assent without hesitation.

To finish his tour, the Major went to check on the bathroom, as he knew from experience that it was always a busy spot at parties. He cut short his visit, however. The sight of a fully dressed man lying in a bathtub of freezing water with a dog was usually enough to put him off his stride.

The ringing mechanism of the telephone then set off, reached the chains of his ossicles, and caused the many tiny things that are found in the human ear to vibrate, whereupon he heard it just as he was crossing the entrance hall to return to the dancing area.

CHAPTER III

"Hello? Monsieur Lustalot?"

"Good evening, Monsieur Miqueut," said the Major, having recognized the harmonious tones of his boss.

"Good evening, Monsieur Lustalot. Are you well? Would you mind, say . . . putting Monsieur Pigeon on the line, please?"

"I'll just see if he's here," said the Major.

Pigeon was standing right behind him.

He communicated his absence to the Major with frantic gestures.

The Major waited for a minute or so, and then: "I can't find him, Monsieur," he said. "But you must've gone to some trouble to get your hands on my number . . ." he continued, with the sudden realization of how anomalous was this . . . etc.

"But, er, in short, right . . . I found your number by the switchboard . . . Madame Legeai had noted it down on a piece of paper. This is quite a pickle . . . I needed Pigeon so we could discuss a matter most urgent."

"Isn't it a bit late?" asked the Major.

"Er, indeed, but, in short . . . seeing as he's there, right . . . Well, so be it—I'll call you back in half an hour. Talk soon, good Lustalot."

The Major hung up. Pigeon looked sick as a parrot.

"You should've told him I wasn't here, my old pal . . ."

"No matter," said the Major. "I'm going to sabotage the phone."

He picked up the telephone set and hurled it at the floor. Pigeon kicked the resulting five pieces under a cupboard.

There was instantly a ringing.

"Zuss christ!" exclaimed the Major. "I've not quite wrecked it."

"No, don't worry," said Pigeon. "It's someone at the door."

He opened it. The downstairs neighbor, stuck to the waist in an ornate copper-nickel-zinc alloy chandelier, had come up to complain and to return the chandelier, which was seriously hindering his ability to move, as well as the Zazou who had been playing Tarzan when the chandelier had fallen.

"I believe these are yours!" said the neighbor.

"But . . ." said the Major. "Is that not your chandelier?"

"No," said the neighbor. "I left mine downstairs."

"So!" said the Major. "It must be our chandelier."

The Major thanked his neighbor for this demonstration of probity and offered him a glass of cognac.

"Monsieur," said his neighbor, "I am too full of scorn for you, you and your gang of Zazous, to accept a drink of your impure brews in your company."

"Monsieur," said the Major, "it was not at all my intention to cause you any offense in offering you this alcohol."

"Forgive me," said the neighbor, seizing the glass. "I thought it was grape juice. I'd forgotten what so much cognac in one go looked like."

He downed it in one go.

"Aren't you going to introduce me to that young lady!?" he asked the Major, pointing at a fat girl who was crossing the entrance hall. "I'm Juste Métivier."

The young lady in question compliantly allowed herself to be picked up by the panting quadragenarian who, third time round, disappeared down the gaping hole left by the fallen chandelier.

In order to avoid further accidents of this kind, the Major pushed a piece of furniture over the hole. Being a little too small, it too disappeared and landed with a soft thud. The Major then tried an original Lapland wardrobe that the uncle had taken care to store in an icebox and which married the exact shape of the hole perfectly.

He went off to look for Lhuttaire, as a pretty voice with blue eyes had asked him where he was. He felt somewhat upset at being unable to spend as much time as he would like with his dear fiancée, but she was dancing so joyfully with Hyanipouletos, Claude Abadie's guitarist, that he didn't have the heart to interrupt her.

In the corridor, a long queue of young men was waiting at the door of the room where Gruyer had been hiding.

The first guy in the queue, armed with a periscope, was scanning the room within through a dynamite-inflicted opening above the door. The Major recognized the man as Lhuttaire.

Relieved, he himself had a look. And on his enthusiastic command, the four guys in the queue rushed as one into the room.

The sound of a bittersweet discussion (the bitter half being Gruyer's) and the whining voice of a young woman who claimed, contrary to all appearances, that she was sleepy, were accompanied by the protests of the four young men, who were saying that their only desire was to have a quiet game of bridge. Before them was an individual with frizzy hair, glasses, no trousers, and shirt standing out proudly at the front. The four intruders left the room, grumbling. When the door shut behind them, the second-in-line took his turn with the periscope.

The Major harpooned Lhuttaire, who had joined the back of queue.

"People are asking where you are!" he told him.

"Whereabouts?" asked Lhuttaire.

"Thereabouts!" said the Major.

"I'm on it!" said Lhuttaire, and he ran off in the opposite direction, dragging the Major with him.

In the bathroom, the dog, tired, was shaking himself vigorously on the rubber bathmat. The man in the bath had just fallen asleep and his breathing created a small whirlpool in the water which grew warmer on contact with his body.

They combed their hair in the mirror without waking him. Then, carefully, they pulled the plug on the bath and left the sleeper high and dry. His clothes were now steaming and little by little the steam filled the room.

They left the bathroom, followed by the dog who had some difficulty in walking, and headed off, chatting about films, to see what was afoot.

At the end of the corridor, the Major was hit full in the face by a mayonnaise sandwich which was flying gleefully through the air, whistling like a blackbird as it went.

"Hayakawa ...'s happenin"!?" he concluded, his rant about Japanese cinema cut suddenly to a close.

Lhuttaire picked up the sandwich and threw it *con brio* whence it seemed to have emanated. He realized, with immediate effect, what a marvelous impact mayonnaise can have on long, ginger hair.

The Major's comb, quite forgiving, smoothed out the mixture, and he and Lhuttaire dashed toward the projectile's original target. Roughly, they squeezed the nose of this smelly individual, and then, each grabbing the redheaded woman by an arm, they found a comfortable corner and enjoyed a half-hour of innocent games.

CHAPTER IV

The frenzy of the Zazous, full of cognac, seemed to be accentuated by nightfall. Dripping with sweat, couples were covering miles and miles, at speed, embracing each other, licking each other, propelling each other, catching each other, twisting each other, untwisting each other, playing leap-frog, piggy-wig, billy-goat, grass-hopper, dragonfly, sewer rat, touch-me-here, just-like-that, budge-your-foot, lift-your-ass, move-your-legs, come-to-me, get-off-me, swearing in English (UK and US), Pidgin, like Hottentots, Coldentots, Bulgarians, Patagonians, Terrafuegans, hex hetera. They all had frizzy hair, they were all wearing white socks and trousers that were tight at the bottom, and they were all smoking light-tobacco cigarettes. The stupidest of them looked mightily disdainful, as one would expect, and the Major's mind was inundated with interesting thoughts on the economic cushioning effect of mattresses filled with banknotes vis-à-vis kicks in the thingy, as he examined with interest the combined entrechats of a dozen tousled enthusiasts. To liven things up, he opened a few more bottles and poured himself a big one. He got a good eyeful by drowning his glass eye and, his gaze sparkling more than ever, he launched himself at a young girl.

Zizanie had left the room accompanied by Hyanipouletos.

However, the Major, swinging into action, was bothered by loud banging on the front door.

It was two more representatives of law and order. An oak lead-lined flowerpot in the shape of a great eagle had just landed on their heads. The recycling center for non-ferrous metals was only fifty meters away and so they were angry, as they saw their job as keeping law and order and not as having to cart lead around.

"You're quite right!" said the Major. "Would you give me just one minute . . . ?"

He headed to the balcony to find Peter Gna, a little worn out by his most recent efforts, smoking a restful cigarette.

The Major grabbed him by his collar and belt and threw him off the balcony. He then threw his sheepskin jacket after him to keep him warm, and a girl to keep him company, before returning to look after his new guests.

"A little brandy?" he asked them, out of habit.

"Gladly," replied the two gendarmes as one voice. It was the voice of duty.

After two bottles, they felt better.

"Would you like me to introduce you to some young women?" the Major asked them.

"A thousand apologies," said the fat one, who had a ginger mustache. "But, as they say, by vocation we're paid arrests."

"Do you operate as a team?" the Major enquired.

"Well . . . Just this once, I suppose we could rough it a little . . . or rough a little one up!" said the thin one, whose Adam's apple looked like a rat in a stovepipe.

The Major called over two Zazous who were studying under the great Maurice Escande of the Théâtre National and placed them in the gendarmes' charge.

"You're under arrest!" said the gendarmes. "Come with us for a good beating . . ."

They disappeared into a broom cupboard, which came highly recommended by the Major. Broom handles come in handy during a power outage and floor polish works as a good substitute.

Increasingly satisfied with the success of his surprise party, the Major launched a raid on the bathroom, gave a dry towel to Hyanipouletos who had just reappeared and whose trousers had begun to stick, and set off in search of Pigeon, while Claude Abadie's band, having recovered their guitarist, were really going for it.

The Major found Emmanuel in one of the back bedrooms. He was convulsed with laughter at the sight of three abominably drunk Zazous relieving themselves into two hats: one in front and one behind.

The Major paid no heed to this rather current phenomenon and instead opened the window because of the smell, threw the Zazous and the hats into the courtyard, and sat himself next to

Emmanuel, who was now coughing, as he had been laughing so hard.

He patted him on the back.

"So, old pal. Are you having a good time?"

"Couldn't be better!" said Emmanuel. "Never laughed so much in my life. The company's very tasteful. Very distinguished. My compliments."

"And have you," enquired the Major, "found a slipper that fits your foot?"

"Generally speaking, I don't do it with my foot, but I feel moved to admit that I have used it to give a good old kick to . . ."

"To?" asked the Major.

"I might as well come straight out with it," said Emmanuel. "To your fiancée."

"You had me going, there, for a second!" said the Major. "I thought you were going to say you'd injured the dog."

"That's what I'd thought too!" said Emmanuel. "It was only afterward that I realized . . ."

"I have to admit she has a funny figure!" said the Major. "But, anyhow, I'm glad you liked her."

"You're a cool guy!" exclaimed Pigeon. Come to think of it, his breath was somewhat reminiscent of the atmosphere in a Hennessy distillery (Cognac, in the Charente region).

"Why not come for a walk round?" suggested the Major. "I'd like to find Antioch."

"You mean you don't know where he is?" asked Emmanuel, astonished.

"No . . ."

"He's asleep in the room next door."

"He's no fool, that one!" warranted the Major, full of admiration. "It's locked, I suppose."

"It is," said Emmanuel. "And he's on his own," he added, enviously.

"Lucky sod," murmured the Major. "Well, come for a walk round, all the same. We'll let him sleep."

In the corridor, they were met by Lhuttaire.

"You won't believe it," he said. "I've just been watching Gruyer. He's really getting stuck in. Up to the wrist . . . He couldn't pull his hand out quick enough. If he had, he'd have smashed me in the face with a bottle. But what a sight!"

"You might have waited for us!" said the Major. "What fun thing do you expect us to do now?"

"We could always go for a drink," said Lhuttaire.

"Let's go."

In the entrance hall, they halted as they thought they could hear someone calling.

It was coming from the front door.

"That's Miqueut's voice!" murmured the Major . . . Emmanuel disappeared like a puff of smoke, sprinted for his life down the corridor, and ended up straddling the toilet's cistern in a fetal position, niftily camouflaging himself with an old slipper.

The Major thought very quickly.

He opened the door.

"Good evening, Monsieur Lustalot," said Miqueut. "Are you well?"

"Thank you, Monsieur," said the Major. "And you?"

"Er . . . well, currently, on the Consortium telephone line, I have a member of the Lost Wrapper Committee, and I wanted to ask Pigeon for a few bits of information . . . That's why I've come to bother you . . . Ha . . . Ha."

"Go and look for him!" said the Major to Lhuttaire, with a wink. "Come this way, Monsieur," he said to Miqueut. "You'll be more comfortable."

Between the bathroom and the cupboard in which the two gendarmes were still working on Escande's students, there was a storage room. It contained just two chairs and a poultice that was past its use-by date.

The Major escorted Miqueut in.

"It's nice and quiet, here," he told him.

He gave him a gentle push in.

"I'll send Pigeon in to see you, right away."

He double locked the door and immediately lost the key.

CHAPTER V

At 2:30 in the morning, the party was in full swing. The Zazous were split into two groups of equal size: those who were dancing and those who were messing around. The latter were scattered willy-nilly throughout the rooms of the apartment, on beds, on sofas, in wardrobes, under furniture, behind furniture, behind doors, under the piano (of which there were three), on the balconies (with blankets), in corners, under rugs, on top of wardrobes, under beds, in beds, in bathtubs, in umbrella stands, here and there, on both sides, in single pile, and in other places, all over the place. Those who were dancing had gathered in just one room, where the band was playing.

Claude Abadie stopped playing at about 3:00. He was due to go and watch the oval ball match the next day between the

Gas-Powered Truckers and the Narrow-Gauge Rail Workers—road versus rail whore-liers—and he planned to get some sleep.

Vidal dropped his little trumpet, extracted its case from under the derrière of D'Haudyt, who had made two cone-shaped impressions in it, and went to look for Emmanuel. Having kissed the Major on the forehead, he joined the rest of the band who were just about to leave. The Zazous put the record player on again and danced with increased gusto.

Antioch had just woken up and reappeared in the company of the Major.

In the bathroom, the man in the bath stood up, turned on the gas, put the hot tap on, and went back to sleep in the bath, forgetting to light the gas.

Thirty minutes elapsed.

Miqueut, in his cell, became aware of the smell of the gas and his impending demise. Frantically, he pulled a notepad from his pocket, found a pen, and started to write . . .

"1. General scope: (a) Aims of this Nothon. To define the conditions in which a Chief Junior Engineer will die when undergoing asphyxia caused by low-pressure gas lighting . . ."

He was drafting a pre-Nothon in accordance with the Nothon plan . . .

Then, the catastrophe occurred . . .

Two Zazous walked past the bathroom. Some argument over nothing had caused a rift between them. One punched the other in the eye. A veritable boxing match . . . an almighty flash . . . and the building blew up . . .

CHAPTER VI

The Major, sitting on the cobblestones of the courtyard strewn with debris, was dabbing his left eye with a scrap of adhesive plaster.

Beside him, Antioch was humming a blues tune.

They were the only people to survive the disaster. The entire block of buildings had been blown up, and nobody had noticed, as the area around Billancourt was in the process of being bombed.

The Major still had his hat, his underpants, and his glass eye. Antioch had his tie. A few feet away, the rest of their clothes were burning in a smoldering pyre.

The air smelt of the devil and cognac. Dust and detritus fell slowly to the ground in a thick cloud.

Antioch—whose body, previously covered with a luxurious coat of hair, was now gleaming, as smooth as a mackintosh skin—was deep in thought, rubbing his chin.

Then the Major spoke.

"When it comes down to it," he said, "I'm not sure I'm cut out for marriage . . ."

"I'm not sure, either . . ." said Antioch.

END

Terry Bradford teaches French, translation and interpreting, at the University of Leeds, in the North of England. Beyond literary translation, his research interests embrace the translation of song (e.g. Jacques Brel) and *bande dessinée* (e.g. Hergé/Bucquoy).